HOLD YOU CLOSE

HOLD YOU CLOSE

USA TODAY BESTSELLING AUTHOR
MELANIE HARLOW
NEW YORK TIMES BESTSELLING AUTHOR
CORINNE MICHAELS

Hold You Close

Copyright © 2018 Melanie Harlow & Corinne Michaels
All rights reserved.
ISBN print: 978-1-7323718-3-5

No part of this publication may be reproduced, distributed, or transmitted in any form or by any means including but not limited to, the training, feeding, or creating any use of artificial intelligence, electronic, mechanical, photocopying, recording, or otherwise without the prior written consent of the author.

This book is a work of fiction, created without use of AI technology.. Names, characters, places, and incidents either are products of the author's imagination or are used fictitiously. Any resemblance to actual events or locales or persons, living or dead, is entirely coincidental and beyond the intent of the author or publisher.

Cover: Sarah Sentz, Enchanting Romance Designs
Editing: Nancy Smay, Evident Ink

prologue
LONDON

~ SEVENTEEN YEARS AGO ~

Pinch me.
 Tell me this isn't a dream.
 Tell me the memories of last night—the most unbelievable, most romantic night of my life—are real.
 Carefully rolling onto my side, I prop my head in one hand and study Ian's face as he sleeps. He's gorgeous, even if I can't see the bright blue of his eyes and he isn't giving me that sexy grin, the one he gave me last night before he said, "You have no idea the things I want to do to you. You should tell me to leave."
 Tell him to leave?
 Why did he think we were in this hotel room all by ourselves? Did he really have no clue how long I'd loved him? Did he not know how many nights I'd spent dreaming that he'd see me as something other than his little sister's best friend? Couldn't he see the way I idolized him? Especially last night . . . he was my hero.
 Back home after his freshman year at UNLV, Ian witnessed my tearful meltdown yesterday morning as I cried to Sabrina that my

1

senior prom date had ditched me last minute for someone else. He offered to take me instead.

I was stunned. He'd kissed me once at a party a couple months back, but we'd hardly spoken since. I figured he'd forgotten all about it.

I'd never felt as beautiful as I did walking into the prom on his arm. Pressed against him as we danced, I'd never felt my heart pound so hard. When he kissed me on the dance floor and told me he'd had feelings for me for a while, I'd never felt so head over heels.

After the dance, he asked me if I wanted to go to the hotel with the rest of my friends. "Yes," I said, forcing myself to be brave. "But I don't want to go to the party. I want to be alone with you." Without another word, he took my hand and we raced for his car. When we arrived at the hotel, Ian got us our own room.

On the elevator, my pulse raced with anticipation. He kept my hand in his as we ascended, and my stomach ballooned as if we were cresting the top of a rollercoaster.

Alone in our room, door locked, shades drawn, lights low, he reached for me. Pulled me against his body. Kissed me as if he knew how many nights I'd dreamed he would.

Tell him to leave?

Not in a million years.

Instead, I gave him everything. My heart, my soul, my body. He was slow and tender and sweet with me, because he knew it was my first time. I was in awe of him—of his hard muscles, of the way he moved, of the thrilling words he whispered.

God, you're so fucking beautiful. I've wanted this for so long. You feel so good.

I still can't believe he wants me. Me! I look nothing like the blond Barbie dolls he usually dates. My hair is dark, my chest is small, and my waist is not the size of my thigh. On a scale of one to ten, most days I feel like a six.

But last night he made me feel like I was the only girl in the entire world. It was magical . . . and it was only the beginning.

Light is spilling in beneath the drapes, so I know it's morning and we should probably get up, especially since Sabrina's graduation party is later this afternoon. I promised to help her with decorations.

But I never want this time with him to end.

He's lying on his back, one arm flung over his head, the sheets pulled up to his waist. I resist the urge to run my hands over his taut abs and muscular chest, but it's not easy.

His eyes open. Upon seeing me, his lips tip up. "Hey."

My heart races. "Hey."

"Did you sleep?"

"A little."

"I didn't tire you out enough?"

I grin. "You did. But it's hard for me to sleep when I'm this excited."

He cocks one eyebrow. "And what has you so excited?"

"You," I say guilelessly. "This. Us."

He grins too. "Come here." Hooking me with both arms, he pulls me tightly against his side, and I lay my head on his chest.

For a moment, I simply breathe him in and let pure happiness wash over me. "Did you mean all those things you said last night?"

"Of course I did. Do you think I'm the kind of asshole who'd lie to you just to get you in bed?"

"I don't know."

"I'm not, London. Look, I might not be the most sensitive guy on the planet, but I'm not a total dick, and I don't take this lightly. We've known each other too long."

"So . . . what happens now?"

He's quiet a moment. "What do you want to happen?"

"I want us to be together." I take a deep breath. "I'm in love with you, Ian."

He freezes, and for a moment I fear I've gone too far.

"You don't have to say it back to me," I say quickly, picking up my head so he can see my face. I want him to know my feelings don't come with any demands. "I just want you to know how I feel."

His eyes are locked on mine. "I've never been in love before."

"I haven't either."

"But the way I feel about you—I've never felt anything like it."

I can't stop a smile from forming. "Really?"

"Really. I want to protect you. Keep you safe." He pauses. "But I also want to fuck you like a hundred and ten different ways. It's actually kind of weird."

I giggle as my stomach whooshes. "A hundred and ten?"

"At least." Suddenly he flips me onto my back so he's on top of me. "And that's just this morning."

My heart threatens to burst from my chest. "I'm not going anywhere."

"Good."

Sex is even better the second time. It doesn't hurt as much, although I'm sore from last night, and I even have an orgasm, thanks to his patience and skill. I'm curious about how many girls he's been with, but I don't really want to know. The only thing that matters is that we're together now. And I hope we always will be.

Mrs. Ian Chase.

London Marie Chase.

Mr. and Mrs. Ian Matthew Chase.

"This feels so right, doesn't it?" I ask dreamily. We're still breathing hard, our skin hot and sticky, his chest heavy on mine.

"Yes."

"Like it was always meant to be."

He props himself up and looks down at me. "Maybe it was."

"So were you just pretending to be annoyed with me all those years Sabrina and I followed you around?"

He shakes his head. "No. You were definitely annoying."

I push against his chest playfully. "You're so mean."

"But you love me, remember?" He drops a kiss on my lips,

then lowers his head to whisper in my ear. "And I love you. It just took me longer to realize it."

A lump forms in my throat, and for a second I'm scared I'm going to embarrass myself by crying. But after a few deep breaths, I'm okay again. More than okay, actually—I'm a new person. Everything is different now. My entire life is him.

"God, I'm so happy, Ian. This changes everything."

"It does?"

"Yes." I'm smiling again.

He picks up his head and looks down at me. "I don't want you to change, London. You're perfect just the way you are."

"I mean my life—it's going to be different now."

"Different how?"

"Well, for one thing, I won't be going to Northwestern in the fall."

He looks confused. "You won't?"

"No, silly. I want to be with you."

He brushes the hair back from my face. "What about that scholarship?"

I shrug. "I got one to UNLV too. I'll take that offer instead."

"But UNLV isn't your dream school. Northwestern is."

"You're my dream. I don't care about anything else."

He doesn't say anything for a moment, and his expression has changed. There's something in his eyes I can't read.

But then he kisses me once more. "Come on. We better get going."

We drag ourselves out of bed and get dressed.

On the short ride home, I alternate between replaying every delicious moment from the night before and fantasizing about everything yet to come. Ian is silent too, and I wonder if he's doing the same.

When he pulls into the driveway of the house I share with my dad, he gets out of the car and walks me to the front door.

"See you in a few hours," I say. "Thanks for . . . everything."

"You're welcome. I'll see you at the party."

I let myself into the house and float dreamily up the stairs, humming a song we danced to last night.

"London?" my dad calls from the second-floor bedroom he uses as an office. "That you?"

"It's me." I pause in the doorway and see him hunched over his computer. The poor man has terrible posture.

"Did you have a good time?" he asks.

"Yes. A wonderful time."

"Good." He smiles at me briefly before focusing on the screen again. It's nothing new—my dad has always been a workaholic. We have that in common. I don't know who was more proud the day I got the scholarship offer from Northwestern, him or me. He's going to take the news hard when I tell him I've decided not to accept it.

But I don't care, I think stubbornly as I continue down the hall to my room. The only thing that matters to me now is being with Ian. I might be only seventeen, but I swear I've loved Ian Chase since the day I met him.

This is the real thing.

～

The party begins at six, and Ian still hasn't shown up. Mrs. Chase keeps asking Sabrina where he is because he's not answering his phone, but neither she nor I have any idea. By seven I start to worry he might be avoiding me. By eight, I'm convinced of it.

"Stop worrying," Sabrina tells me. We're in her bedroom sharing a strawberry wine cooler we snuck upstairs. She takes a sip and hands it to me. "He'll be here eventually."

"I just have a bad feeling." I take a few swallows of the sweet fizzy drink.

"Why? He said all the right things, didn't he?"

"Yes," I admit.

"Then I'm sure he's just being his usual clueless self. I love my brother and all, but he rarely thinks about anyone's feelings besides his own. He probably has no idea he's making you worry."

"Maybe you're right." I force a smile, take another sip, and hand the bottle back to her. "Sorry. I'm being stupid. Let's finish this and go back to your party."

By the time the bottle is empty, I've got a happy little buzz going and I feel much better. But as soon as we come out of the house, I nearly throw up. Because that's when I see him kissing another girl in the backyard.

I can't breathe. My stomach churns. My clothes feel too tight.

Sabrina grabs my hand. "Hey. Let's go back inside."

I shake her off. "No."

"Lon, come on. He's just a jerk, okay? Let's go sneak another wine cooler."

How could he?

I don't understand. He lied to me. He said he loved me and now he's touching another girl? After everything we had last night and this morning? I want to scream. Cry. Throw something.

But instead of any of those things, I march over to where he's standing with a pretty blonde wearing tiny denim shorts and a red bikini top. She fills it out in a way I never could.

I feel like pushing her into the pool. Him, too.

"Ian, can I talk to you for a minute?" I'm surprised at how calm I sound. Inside, I'm falling apart.

He looks at me with zero emotion on his face. Like last night didn't even happen. "Oh, hey London. This is Heidi. She goes to UNLV with me."

Heidi gives me a bored look. "Hi."

Ignoring her, I skewer Ian with my eyes. "You brought a date?"

He shrugs heartlessly. "I guess you could call it that."

My heart is racing, and I think I might pass out. I've never felt this before. Is it normal for your chest to physically ache? Because each breath I take hurts.

"Wait a minute." I hold up my hands, my eyes filling with

tears. "What is this? I thought you meant what you said last night. And this morning."

Heidi giggles, which makes me want to throat punch her, and I'm not even sure what throat punching is. "God, Ian, what did you say to this poor girl?"

Ian looks me right in the eye and breaks my heart in three words. "It was nothing."

All at once it's clear I've been a total idiot. How could I have thought he was really interested in me? I'm a pathetic little kid with a crush. He doesn't love me. I gave him exactly what he wanted, and now I'm worthless.

I hate him. I hate myself for believing him and thinking I should throw my life away.

"Fuck you," I whisper. Then I turn around and run, vowing I will never, ever let anyone hurt me this way again.

Especially him.

As I stumble around the side of the house, I thank God I didn't tell my father I wanted to turn down the offer from Northwestern. All I want now is to get the hell away from Ian Chase.

The farther the better.

CHAPTER ONE

ian

"The line to get in is crazy," my manager, Drea, says as I'm going over last night's sales figures. "We're over capacity as it is."

"Uh huh," I say, not looking up from the screen.

I don't care about the line. I don't care about people waiting to get into the club, I care about money. Veil is the hottest nightclub in Vegas right now, and I damn sure plan to keep it that way.

"Ian." She taps the desk.

"Okay, great, what do you want me to do?" I ask.

"I don't know, but we're going to get fined again."

I huff, and lean back in my chair. "Then fix the issue."

She pulls her long blond hair to the side, leaning forward on my desk so her fake boobs are extra—large. My eyes go there, I can't help it, they're in my damn face. "Not going to work," I tell her, slowly bringing my gaze to her pouty lips. Drea gets what she wants by using her ... assets ... to bend men to her will. I've seen it in action and it's impressive, but she's barking up the wrong tree. I'm a man of principle and honor.

Well, that's a lie, but I have no interest in shitting where I eat, at least.

"Ugh," she groans. "You're the only man in Vegas who won't sleep with me, or at least do what I want."

I laugh. "I'm the only smart man you've met then," I challenge.

She's tried, God knows she has, but I prefer to keep my dipstick out of the lube at work. Now, the patrons, they're all fair game.

"Or the only man who doesn't have a brain," she retorts.

I won't even dignify that with a response. I've learned over the years that Drea needs to be wanted. The only thing I want is for her to be the manager I need. "Do your job, Drea, and deal with it."

Her lips turn down and I can sense this isn't going to go my way. "Can you please smooth this over with the cops?" she asks.

I close my eyes, pinching the bridge of my nose. "The cops are here?"

"That's how I know it's a problem," she tosses back at me.

I get to my feet, irritated that she failed to mention that. The last thing Veil needs is another run-in with the cops. I've had enough fines, warnings, and calls to break up fights to last me a lifetime. I also prefer to keep them out of my establishment as much as possible.

"Lead with that next time," I instruct and stroll out.

The club is alive. Everyone is dancing, drinking, spending their money, and I couldn't be happier. My parents thought I was nuts for opening the club, but I had a hunch. My sister was the only one who backed me. She was the most vocal about getting my head out of my ass and doing something "real" with my life, and supported me one-hundred percent when I said this is what I wanted to do. My parents hoped that meant becoming an accountant, but after spending almost ten years as a promoter, I knew the ins and outs of the club life. I took the money I'd saved up and bought Veil. The location on the strip is prime, and it paid off.

My sister smiled at my parent's disapproval, as did I.

As I walk around the club, I say hello to some of the girls who come often. Getting them in the door once is great, but when they come back, that's a win. I'm definitely winning right now.

"Ian," my bartender, Toby, calls with his hand out.

"What's up?"

"You have a call." He pushes the phone toward me.

No one calls the club for me other than vendors, and it's eleven-thirty at night, so whoever it is can wait.

"I have to deal with something now, send them to my voicemail."

He shakes his head. "She's called three times." The annoyance in his voice is clear, even over the music.

She?

The only woman that would resort to calling the club is my ex-wife. God only knows what bullshit she wants now. For all I know she broke a nail, it's my fault, and she thinks I should pay for her new manicure, or a hand replacement. She's like the gift you've tried to return but can't find the receipt for, so you're stuck with it. I hate unwanted presents, and I hate Jolene.

"Send the devil to my voicemail," I say and walk away.

I head out to the sidewalk. Drea wasn't kidding, the line is nuts. "Hello, Officer," I say to the pudgy cop standing next to the bouncer.

"Mr. Chase, we're getting complaints," he says, looking down the sidewalk at the line.

"I can't help that we're popular." I shrug. "I'm at capacity, and can't kick out the paying customers to take care of the line."

"You're obstructing the entrances of other businesses because of the way your overflow lines are set up."

How the hell would they like me to handle it? We're not inside the casino, there's no way to control the line. I'm not about to turn away people when we hit the number ten. This is a business, and part of the free marketing I get is thanks to the line.

"All right, I'll figure something out." I grip the back of my neck.

I feel my phone vibrate in my pocket. If this is Jolene, I swear to God, I might lose my fucking mind.

The name flashes across the screen, London Parish. For fuck's sake. Like I need to deal with my sister's uptight, irritating best friend right now. London would be incredibly hot if she wasn't such a raging bitch. I look at my call log and see this is the third time she's called.

I walk down the strip a little, and after a few deep breaths, I call her back.

"Ian, you need to come to my house."

I smirk. "Well, this is a first. Did you have the stick removed from your ass?"

"Don't. Not today, please. Just come here." I hear her sniff and my protectiveness kicks in. Someone made her cry. We don't get along at all—partly because we're polar opposites and partly because of our history—but no one gets to make her cry.

"Are you hurt?" I ask.

"Not in the way you think." Her voice hitches.

I've known London for twenty-five years. I can count on one hand how many times I've seen or heard her cry—I was the reason one of those times.

"What's wrong? Is it an emergency? Because I'm at work and the club—"

"Now, Ian. You need to come here now."

She also doesn't play games.

Fuck.

I look at my watch and blow a deep breath through my nose. It'll take me at least thirty minutes to get there. This is seriously a shitty night. "I'll be there as soon as I can."

"Just... hurry," London says and hangs up.

Dread pulls at my stomach, telling me there's something going on. I don't know what, but I know I need to get there.

"Get rid of the line, no more get in," I tell the bouncer, and then head inside.

Drea is at the bar, and my anxiety is starting to grow. London needs me there, why? What happened? Did someone break into her house? Mine? Maybe it has to do with an ex, if she even has one, or it could be nothing like that. Regardless, her voice was shaky and I can't waste time wondering.

"I have to go," I tell Drea.

Her eyes widen. "Go? Go where? It's a packed house."

"I'm aware of that, but something came up. I need you to handle things tonight." I turn to Toby. "Stay until Drea is done closing and I want you to escort her to her car at the end of the night."

He nods.

I never let her walk out of here alone. Even if I have someone coming home with me, Drea's not going to be unescorted. Too many men get the wrong impression because she's nice to them. Over my dead body will she be hurt as a result of working at my club.

After I get in the car, my mind is racing. I drive faster than I should, telling myself that London is just being dramatic.

And then I remember ... she has my nephew and nieces at her house.

My foot pushes down on the pedal of my Jaguar, making the engine howl with each mile. I turn into the development where we both live, pass my house, and head to hers. I still hate that our backyards touch. Every damn day I see her sitting out on her deck, reading her books, looking down at me with her disapproving attitude.

When I get there, the flashing lights of a police car brighten the road. I don't think. I don't know if I even put the car in park before I'm out of the vehicle.

"London!" I yell as I rush through the door. "Christopher? Morgan? Ruby?" I call out for the kids, praying it's not one of them.

When I get to the living room, I release a heavy sigh—they're all there, not hurt.

Then I see the tears streaming down Morgan's face. London

gets to her feet. Her eyes are red, puffy, and black mascara runs down her cheeks. "Ian." She chokes on my name.

"What's wrong? What happened?"

The girls start to cry again, and my nephew pulls them into his arms.

London moves toward me, placing her hand on my chest. "They're gone."

"Who?" I ask, confused.

"Sabrina and David," she whispers.

Yeah, they went on a trip. Why the hell are they crying? "This is what you called me for? They'll be home in a few days. Why are you crying too?" I ask.

Her green eyes meet mine and her lips part. "No." She shakes her head. "They won't."

I look over at the kids again, and then to the muted television. My feet move closer, because I have to be sure the words flashing across the screen say what I think they say. "Flight 1184 crashes off the coast of Hawaii. Three hundred missing and presumed dead."

My sister was going to Hawaii.

My sister is gone.

I sink to my knees in front of the kids, unsure what to say. They just lost their parents, and my heart is breaking. My sister was my best friend. She was the one who pushed me to open Veil and do what I wanted. I've always had her support, and now she's gone.

Christopher lifts his head, his brown eyes filled with unshed tears. "They'll find them," he says with conviction.

"Okay," I reply. We both know it's a lie, but it's one he has to tell himself. I remember being fifteen; there was no telling me I was wrong.

"Dad wouldn't..." he starts, and then stops as his lip quivers.

My own tears start to fall, as Morgan grabs my hand. "What do we do now?"

I have no fucking clue. How do I tell these kids how to survive?

I'm the last person in the world equipped to give this advice. I look to London. Her hand touches my shoulder and she wipes the tears that fall silently down her cheeks.

"We hold each other close," she says.

Our eyes meet and I'm transported back to a time when London and I weren't always at each other's throats. A time when we had feelings for each other. Even though we're both aching, there's something keeping us from breaking completely—a trust that even in the deepest pain, we can still come together and offer comfort.

London kneels beside me. She looks like she's on the verge of falling apart, but won't allow it to happen. "Did you call my parents?" I ask.

"They're getting on a plane."

The five of us huddle together and soothe each other, as we all realize our lives will never be the same again.

CHAPTER TWO

ian

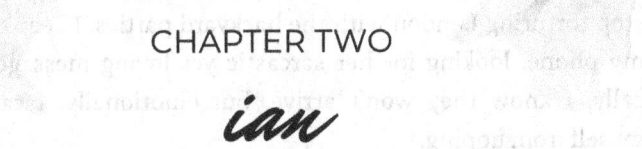

Today, we buried two empty caskets in the Las Vegas desert. It's been two weeks and no survivors have been found. Neither my brother-in-law's nor my sister's body has been recovered. But my parents thought it would be best to give the kids some sense of closure and have the services.

Whatever that means.

How do you close a door to your parents?

"Uncle Ian?" Christopher calls for my attention.

"How are you holding up, man?"

At fifteen, I wouldn't have been able to act the way he has. He's been a pillar of strength for his sisters.

For the first time, I see a crack in his armor. "I don't know how to do this," he admits. "I don't know how to go back to the house today. They're really not coming back."

The first night, we all stayed at London's. No one slept, and all of us were lost in a sea of grief. When Mom and Dad got here, they took the kids back to their own house so they could sleep in their beds.

"One day at a time, Chris. That's all any of us can do, but I'm always here, you know that." I tell him.

He nods. "I keep waiting for Dad to walk in the door. But now ..."

I know the feeling. Each day, Sabrina would text me, telling me something I needed to do better with my time or telling me to stop torturing London with the backyard parties. I keep checking my phone, looking for her sarcastic yet loving messages. Logically, I know they won't arrive, but emotionally, I can't stop myself from hoping.

"I hope you know how much they loved you," I tell him.

Christopher looks at me and a tear falls. "I know, it's why this hurts so bad."

"You're going to get through this," I say to both him and myself.

I miss my sister.

Sabrina was the best person I knew. She picked my sorry ass up when Jolene fucked with my head. Even David, who I fucking hated for knocking up my sister in college, became a brother to me.

He did right by her, took care of her, provided a life for her and their kids. I admired him, and I don't know that I ever told him that.

Now I never will.

So many goddamn regrets.

"Do you think we'll have to move to Florida?" Christopher asks.

My mother tried to bring that up last night, but I wasn't in the right mindset to discuss it. Talking about all of it was too much. The idea of not seeing the kids anymore after losing Sabrina is a road I can't go down.

I don't claim to be the world's best uncle, but I love those three. I'm the one who buys them the cool thing their parents won't let them have. When I show up on Christmas, it's clear who Santa Claus really is—me. I'm their godfather, all three of them are mine in some way. I spoil the shit out of them, teach them things they should know, and love them with my whole heart.

I'm well aware of what people think about me. I'm divorced, drive a sports car, own a nightclub, and get laid whenever I want, but that doesn't mean things don't bother me. I'll never have kids, so they're it for me.

"I really don't know what's going to happen." I give it to him straight.

Right then my mother walks over. "We're all going to follow the lawyer back to his office." She touches Chris's arm. "All of us, Ian."

"I have to get back to the club."

She gives me the look that makes even grown men shit themselves when they see it. The eyes that demand you listen. "The lawyer stated that you, London, living parents, and the children were to be at the reading of the will."

Even in death, Sabrina is in charge.

I open my mouth to refuse. I have a business to run and Drea is really not as capable as I'd like her to be. We've only been open four months, and I can't screw this up.

"Please, Uncle Ian," Chris pleads.

Well, shit. I can't say no now. This is my first godson. The one I hoped to corrupt and teach to drive his mother to drink. He's supposed to become my protégé, and I can't let him down.

"All right, I'll be there." I clasp his shoulder and walk to the car.

"Thanks."

London walks over with huge black sunglasses on her face, but they don't disguise her grief. She has had no problem shedding tears. I've never seen her cry as much as I have in the last five days. I had to lock myself down to keep from trying to comfort her with each sob she released. She's made it clear, however, that I'm not the person she seeks out when she's in pain.

I've managed to keep it together for now. Mostly because my father always taught me that when the women are struggling, they need the men to carry the weight. So he's helping Mom, and I've got the kids.

He and I share a look as my mother starts crying again. I hear him in my head. *"Men are fixers, Son. Men are strength. Men don't let anyone see vulnerability. When someone hurts your mother or sister, you'll fight. If someone you love is in pain, you fight, got it?"*

Those words were drilled into me, and every part of me wants to fight, but there's no one to battle. I wish there was.

"Can I ride with you? I don't have my car," London explains.

Under normal circumstances, London would never ask to go anywhere with me. And if she did, I would throw out some smartass remark or give her crap about it, but since we lost Sabrina, neither of us has taken a single jab at the other. Part of me wants to pick a fight with her just to have something be the way it was before.

But I can't do that.

"Fine." I start walking toward my car, and she falls in step beside me, her arms crossed over her chest. Her dark hair is twisted up in that strict-librarian style she always wears. She should wear it down more often.

"Have you seen the will?" she asks.

"No."

"What do you think will happen with the kids?"

I shrug, irritated that she brought up the one subject I'm trying to avoid thinking about. "My parents will probably get them."

"Will they take them back to Florida?"

"How should I know?" My tone is a little too sharp, and I feel like an asshole for being rude to her today. She and I have our issues, which are not entirely my fault, as she would like to believe, but she loves those kids—she's their godmother. They call her "Aunt London," and she was there the day each one of them was born.

She looks over at me. "It was just a question, Ian. I thought maybe your sister had talked to you about it."

"Well, she didn't."

"Maybe if you spent a little less time partying at the club and more time with your family, she would have."

There's the London I know. Maybe she wants a fight too. *Happy to oblige, sweetheart.*

"It's my fucking job, London. I'm working, not partying." We reach the car and I unlock it with the fob in my pocket before opening the passenger door for her.

She pauses, looks at my hand on the door and then up at me. "Only you could be a dick and a gentleman at the same time."

"It's a gift," I tell her. "Now get in. I've got things to do today."

With a roll of her eyes, she gets into my car and I shut the door after her. As I walk around to the driver's side, I wipe the sweat from my forehead. It's warm for April, almost ninety today, and I wish more than anything I could spend the afternoon at the pool in my backyard, a cold beer in my hand and a sexy blonde in the chair next to me. Maybe two blondes. One on either side.

I wish I could blow off work and drink all day and play loud music and mess around with the blondes in full view of London, and she'd call me to complain I was being completely obnoxious, but I'd ignore her, so she'd call my sister and bitch about my disgusting behavior and my complete disregard for my neighbors' Sunday peace and quiet. My sister would text me to please quit being a jerk and consider other people's feelings, by which she'd mean London's feelings, and I'd say it wasn't my fault London was a crusty old maid with only her cat for company, and maybe if she wasn't such a bitter, puritanical goody-goody, she'd come over and join the fun instead of stewing about it from her deck and tattling on me.

I wish a lot of things.

I wish I could change the past. I wish my sister was still alive. I wish her kids still had a mother and father. I wish I knew how to answer questions about their future and how any of us are supposed to move on.

"I saw Jolene," London says, probably just to annoy me. Which it does.

I pull onto the highway, grunting in response. I saw my ex among the crowd, wearing a ridiculous hat and crying fake tears, but I didn't speak to her.

"It was nice of her to come, don't you think?"

Nothing my ex-wife does is charitable or kind. She's a snake, filled with venom and ready to strike at the first thing she can stick her fangs into. Usually it's me. And speaking of fake—London doesn't like Jolene any better than I do. "No. I don't."

London rolls the window down and grumbles under her breath. "Whatever."

I roll up London's window and turn up the A/C, just to piss her off. "She didn't come to be nice, London. She came to gawk and get gossip so she can be the center of attention at work tomorrow. It's not as if she even liked Sabrina."

"Everybody liked Sabrina." Now it's London whose voice has an edge.

"You know what I mean."

She turns toward the passenger window, giving me the cold shoulder for the rest of the ride.

Fine with me.

But it's true, what she said. Everybody did like my sister. Sabrina didn't have a mean bone in her body, and she always had a smile and something nice to say to anyone, even my shrew of an ex-wife. *Sweet* was a word I heard over and over again today as her friends and family mourned her. Kind-hearted. Generous. Thoughtful.

Did you know she volunteered at the Humane Society?

When my mom passed, she brought dinner over every night for a week.

I can't tell you how much we're going to miss her at work—she was the hardest working nurse on the floor.

I might have had the better grades, higher SAT scores, and more trophies on the shelf, but I'm positive no one ever called Sabrina an asshole, or punched her in the face, or told her she had the emotional sensitivity of a wood chip. She knew how to make people feel good about themselves. She made the world a better place.

Me? I know how to run a club and have a good time. What I make is money.

Which is why I'm stunned half an hour later when the lawyer reads Sabrina's will, in which she's left her children to me.

CHAPTER THREE
London

"I'm sorry—what?" I put a hand in the air to stop the attorney from going on. "Can you repeat that last part?"

One glance across the conference table at Ian tells me he's just as shocked as I am to have heard his name listed as primary guardian of Sabrina's kids. His face has gone pale.

The attorney at the head of the table reads it again. "If my husband does not survive me and I leave minor children surviving me, I appoint as guardian of the person and property of my minor children my brother, Ian Chase. He shall have custody of my minor children, and shall serve without bond. If he does not qualify or for any reason ceases to serve as guardian, I appoint as successor guardian my friend London Parish."

"Wait a minute. Wait a minute." Ian's deep voice fills the room as he rises to his feet, one hand on his chest. "Are you saying she left the kids to me?"

We all glance at the empty chairs where the kids, tearstained and exhausted, had been sitting until a few minutes ago when Christopher volunteered to take his younger siblings to find something to drink. The poor kid is shouldering such a huge burden, trying to be strong for his sisters while dealing with his own grief. And those sweet little girls—Morgan is at that age where she needs her mother more than ever, and darling Ruby has hardly spoken a word since we got the news. My heart aches for them.

"Yes." The attorney looks at Ian. "You weren't aware of her wishes?"

"No. When was this will made?"

The attorney glances down at the paper in his hands. "Actually, it was signed only recently. Last month, in fact. The fifth of March."

"She never said anything to me about it." Ian, clearly agitated, loosens the knot in his tie.

"Or me," I say, trying to wrap my brain around this. Why would Sabrina and David choose Ian, of all people? I was distraught by the thought that her parents might be taking the kids to Florida, but at least I was somewhat *prepared* for that news. This is a total bombshell. I'm torn between feeling glad that the kids won't be leaving and hurt that Sabrina chose her irresponsible, heart-breaking, playboy brother to raise her children instead of me. What kind of example will he be?

"Are you sure it doesn't say Philip Chase?" Sabrina's mother, Nancy, asks. She's gripping her husband's hand with both of hers, and her voice shakes.

"Yes. Look again, please." Silver-haired Philip speaks with the authority of a retired general, and the attorney does as requested.

"No, it says 'my brother Ian Chase.'" He looks at Ian again. "I assume you are her brother?"

"Yes. But I—"

"Ian," Nancy says, looking up at her son. "If you don't want them, we can take them."

"I never said I—"

"I want them," I announce, rising to my feet. "If Ian won't raise them, I will."

"Can everyone just wait one fucking minute?" Ian puts both hands out, one toward his parents and one toward me. In the chair next to me, David's mother gasps. She and David's father are Christian missionaries, and Ian's foul mouth probably offends her. I can't imagine what she'd do if she witnessed the debauchery at one of his pool parties.

"I never said I didn't want the kids," he goes on. "I'm simply digesting the news."

"But Ian," his mother says, dabbing at her eyes with a handkerchief. "You've never had children. You don't know how to take care of them."

"She doesn't have children either." He gestures toward me. "What makes her so qualified?"

Remaining on my feet, I lean forward and brace both hands on the table. Clearly the uneasy truce we've had all week is over. "I love those kids like they're my own. I know everything about them."

"I do, too." His eyes are a piercing blue, and the way he's got them focused on me, like I'm the only person in the room, is unsettling. It drives me insane that I still find him attractive after all these years. I hate it.

"Oh, really?" I challenge. "What grade is Christopher in?"

"Ninth." His expression is smug.

Damn. He got it right. "When's Morgan's birthday?"

He looks a little less sure of himself. "January... tenth?"

Ha! "Twelfth. What does Ruby call her stuffed panda?"

That one stumps him completely.

"Fred," I announce, glaring at him. "She calls him Fred."

Ian runs a hand through his dark blond hair. "Look, just because you've memorized more random facts about them doesn't mean you love them more than I do."

"No, but it means I'm better qualified to raise them. You're a nightclub owner, Ian. Gone all hours. And when you are home..." I let that sentence dangle for a moment.

"What?" he demands, his brow furrowing. "Fucking say it, London."

Another gasp from my left.

I straighten up, lifting my shoulders, determined to show

everyone that I am clearly the better choice. "I'm not sure your home environment is the best one to raise children in, that's all."

"And why's that?"

"You want me to say it? You want me to talk about all the parties and the drinking and the women and the loud music?"

He rolls his eyes, which infuriates me.

"Some people are sleeping at three AM, Ian," I snap.

"Some people don't have lives."

"Some people are as rude and insensitive at thirty-seven as they were at nineteen."

"Some people hold a grudge for way too long."

The attorney clears his throat as Ian and I continue to glare at each other across the table. "Mr. Chase, your sister and brother-in-law wished for you to be the primary guardian of their children. Are you prepared to assume that responsibility?"

"Yes." He never takes his eyes off me.

"Good. Now if you'll both be seated, I'll finish reading the wills."

Neither of us wants to be the one who sits first—it would feel like losing the standoff—but since I have manners (unlike *some* people), I take my seat once more. After tightening the knot in his tie, Ian sits too.

The attorney finishes Sabrina's will and moves on to David's, but my mind keeps wandering. I simply cannot get over the fact that Sabrina and David wanted Ian to raise their children. What were they thinking? Was it because he was blood and I wasn't? But he's irresponsible, stupid, and smug. An overgrown man-child, not father material. Sabrina told me many times that he needed to grow up and stop his partying. Did she think giving him her children was going to magically make him become an adult? They didn't even ask him to watch the kids when they had a date night, let alone when they took a rare trip on their own! There was a reason the children were at my house when that plane went down—Sabrina trusted me to best take care of them.

She knew I loved them like my own. And since it looks like I won't ever have any...

I stop myself from going down that path. This isn't the time.

From across the table, I sense Ian looking at me, and my body grows warm beneath my black suit. I shift uncomfortably in my chair and try to focus my attention on what the attorney is saying about estate taxes and beneficiaries. But a moment later it's all too much, and my throat begins to tighten.

Sabrina is gone. My best friend for the last twenty-five years —since we were ten, and I was the new girl at school without any friends and too shy to say hello to anyone. I sat alone on the bus and fought off tears, feeling the other kids' eyes on me and praying desperately that they wouldn't make fun of my glasses or my lunchbox or my clothing or anything else children can be cruel about.

Then she got on the bus. I knew right away she was well liked by the way kids greeted her. Even the driver called her by name, returning her "good morning" and her smile. Our eyes met, and next thing I knew, she was heading up the aisle and sliding into the seat next to me.

"Hi," she said. "Are you new?"

I nodded.

Her smile grew brighter. Wider. "I'm Sabrina. What grade are you in?"

"Fifth," I managed.

"Same as me." Her eyes were kind—big and blue, and framed by thick black lashes. The same eyes boring into me from across the table, but hers had been far friendlier.

We were inseparable after that. Her best friend had moved to California the previous summer, and we discovered we had a lot in common. Obsessed with boy bands, but still secretly liked to play Barbies. Dying to get our ears pierced but scared of the needle. Curious about boys, but disgusted by the thought of actually kissing one.

Every possible rite of female passage, we went through

together. We told each other everything. We made no decision without asking the other for advice. We traded clothes and books and shoes and secrets.

She was there for me when Ian broke my heart and understood why I had a hard time trusting men after that. I was there for her when she discovered she was pregnant at age twenty, and stood by her side when she married David. I loved her with my whole heart. With tear-filled eyes, I risk a glance across the table.

Ian now gets the very best and only part of her that's left—those kids.

"Do you have any questions?" the lawyer asks, snapping me out of my memories.

"Does the will state anything about her wishes as to where the kids will live? Maybe a letter? An instruction guide?" Ian asks. "My sister was a planner, she had to leave me something telling me what to do."

He's ridiculous. He would know all that if he wasn't so self-absorbed. "She'd want you to live in her house. It's their home." I grip the table. "How could you even think about taking anything else away from them? You need to give them stability."

"I'm asking a question, not making a choice."

"Well, you need to get a clue and a life not centered around yourself." I glare as I spit the words.

"Ironic coming from you. You live alone, with your cat. At least I have a life."

I roll my eyes. "The point is that it's not about you. For some reason, Sabrina thought you'd do the right thing by her kids."

Ian flinches slightly at Sabrina's name. As much as I hate him, I know he loved her. She was our rock in this world. I see how much thinking of her hurts him.

Ian runs his hand down his face. "And you'd move out of your house?"

Without a second thought. "For them? Yes. I'm not worried about myself in this situation."

His jaw ticks as he stares me down. "Obviously, my sister

trusted my judgment or she wouldn't have named me their guardian over some people."

"That's enough!" Nancy yells, pushing her seat back. "You two are all they have right now. Don't you see that? You both have been a part of their lives more than any of us. Those kids are going to be lost and looking to the people they love for support and guidance. If you can't stop this bickering, then it's going to be at my grandchildren's peril." She wipes the tear that descends her cheek. "We're all in pain, but Sabrina and David trusted you, so don't fail them. Stop all this nonsense and focus on what's important."

Nancy is overcome with emotion and leaves the room with Philip following her. Shame floods me as her words sink in. I don't know what to say. Nancy is right. Sabrina chose Ian for some reason, and I have to honor her wishes. I'll still be there for them, loving them just like I would've if she and David were alive. Sabrina never did anything that wasn't in her children's best interest. We have to stop fighting because Chris, Morgan, and Ruby need all the family they have left.

"It's very clear that Mr. and Mrs. Donegan wanted you both to be involved in their children's lives." The lawyer gets to his feet while gathering the papers. "I'll give you both a few minutes to digest everything that's happened today. As for a letter or an instruction guide, she left these and asked that they be read in private. I'll have them for you on your way out." He gathers a stack of envelopes in his hands.

I nod. "Thank you."

He returns the gesture with a soft smile. "I've dealt with this too many times, Ms. Parish and Mr. Chase. Families are torn apart by loss and tragedy, but your sister was a sweet woman. She loved her kids and she loved her brother. She and her husband agonized over this. They truly considered every aspect."

Ian grips the back of his neck. "She got that from my father. He taught us to prepare for any situation and always have a plan."

"Yes, well, it was a good thing he did because we never know what will happen," he says before walking out the door.

We're quiet for a few minutes, letting everything that happened a few minutes ago settle around us. Sabrina wanted her children to go with Ian for some unknown reason. Maybe she explained it in a letter to me? Maybe the answer to what in the world was going through her mind is there. She was a planner, I know this, but it still makes no sense to me.

Ian's eyes meet mine and I see the boy I knew a long time ago. "You can judge me all you want, London, but I love those kids."

"Loving them and being there for them are two different things."

He shakes his head. "I'm not a fucking teenager anymore. You need to get over yourself and what happened between us. Open your eyes and see who I am. I'm a successful business owner with a nice house, and everything I could want. Those kids are my sister's kids and just because you're hung up on who I was once upon a time doesn't mean you know me now."

"I live behind you," I remind him. "I see the life you live. You work insane hours, and who is going to watch the kids when you're at the club until four in the morning?"

Ian stands, moving to the window. "I'll figure it out."

"What about Ruby's dance classes?"

He crosses his arms over his chest. "I'll take her."

"Chris's basketball? What about Morgan's science project that's due next week? Did you even know she was accepted into the advanced science program?" I keep pushing. "Oh, and what about on Saturdays when you'd normally be having your little sleepovers? Are you planning to have Morgan tuck them all in?"

He glares at me. So much anger radiates off of him. "Jealous?"

"Of them? Umm, no." I almost gag. I'm not jealous of them because I would never want to be those girls. I want to be loved, desired, placed above everyone else. I feel bad for them. They'll be tossed out the next morning like trash and a new wave will come in the next weekend.

"Look, London. I just found out that not only did I lose my sister and brother, who were also my fucking best friends, but I now have three kids! Do I have all the answers? No, but I'm a smart guy and I'll manage just fine."

"Great," I huff. He doesn't have a clue what all this means. It's not just some overnight stay, this is the rest of their lives. It's an entirely new way of living, but I'm sure he doesn't even get that yet. He never sees the big picture.

"None of this is great," Ian says, running his hand down his face. "Not a single thing about any of this is great. I shouldn't be taking care of those kids, it should be their mother and father."

Softening, I get to my feet, walk over to where he is, and place my hand on his back. "I'm sorry." My words are full of remorse. "Sabrina was *like* a sister to me, but she was yours."

He turns, his eyes full of emotion. "It doesn't feel real, you know?"

I do. I keep waiting for things that won't ever come. My phone to ring, her to show up at my door because David told her to go do something for herself, a box to end up on my stoop that she ordered and is hiding from David, or my heart to stop hurting. "Look, I don't want to fight with you . . ."

He snorts. "That's all we do."

"It doesn't have to be. I'm not saying I like you or that we'll ever be friends again, but we both love those kids. I want to be there for them, help them through this, and maybe the two of us can give them some hope."

Christopher opens the door. "Aunt London, Uncle Ian?"

"Hi, honey." I watched him become a man in just a few minutes when we found out about the crash. It was an instant switch.

"Ruby is really tired and Morgan won't stop complaining about her cell phone dying. Can we go wherever it is we're going?"

Ian looks to me, and then over to Chris. "Come on in and shut the door."

"I don't think—" I start, but Ian touches my arm.

"Your mom and dad left me as your guardian if something happened to them," he tells Chris. "I want to talk to you, since you're the oldest, and tell you that I would like you three to move into my house. I have plenty of room, the pool, the man cave, and your Aunt London is right in my backyard."

Chris sits, his hands gripped tightly in front of him. "Okay."

"Okay?" I ask. "You don't want to stay in your house?"

He shakes his head. "I don't. It's too hard."

Another sliver of my heart breaks off. "What about the girls?"

Christopher's head drops. "No matter where we live, this is hard."

I touch his cheek. "No one wants to make this harder," I tell him. "If you want to stay in your house, your uncle and I will find a way." I don't care what's on paper; I'm not going to tear another thing away from these kids.

"No, we're going to give the kids a united front," Ian commands from behind me. "I think it's best if they stay in my home for the time being. If we need to make adjustments, we'll do that."

I want to scream at him about once again being a selfish asshole, but I won't do that in front of Chris.

Ian touches his shoulder. "Go get your sisters ready, we'll be out in a minute."

As soon as Chris is gone, Ian's anger is directed back at me.

"Don't do that to them," he warns.

"Do what?"

"Make them assurances you can't give."

"I didn't!"

"So you're agreeing to watch them at night and on the weekends?"

"Umm . . . " My eyes widen. "Who said that?"

"Well, you love those kids, and you just said . . ." He puts his fingers up to make air quotes. "We'll find a way."

"That's not what I meant. I never said I would become their babysitter."

"Why not? I figure you're never busy at night or on a weekend." He shrugs.

"That doesn't mean I'm your new nanny!"

Ian takes a step back, pursing his lips. "True, but you said you'd help. You said you wanted to be there for them. What better way than working out some kind of shared custody? You can be there and I can work. We both win."

"Wait, you want me to share the kids as though we have some kind of custody arrangement?"

He lifts his palms. "You suggested it, I'm merely coming up with an agreement. When the will was read, you seemed pissed that Sabrina didn't leave you the kids, since you're so responsible and I'm not, in your mind."

"You're twisting my words."

"I'm just glad you offered to help."

Ugh. "I didn't! I have a life, I can't watch them every weekend. How is that fair? I would be willing to help, but not every weekend." Is he out of his mind?

Ian smirks. "I'm sure your cat won't mind. And it's not like there's ever a man around, so the kids don't have to worry about your dating life. Seems like a perfect solution."

My jaw drops. "You are such an asshole."

"So you'd rather I hire someone the kids don't know? What if Ruby cries? Or Morgan can't do her homework? You're fine with a stranger coming into their life?" Ian tosses back.

Once again, he's reminded me why I loathe him. This is what we are. We fight. Claw, scratch, and tear each other apart. He's an asshole and I'm a bitch. We bring out the worst in each other. It's been this way since . . . I let him in.

One mistake.

One night.

One thing that will never happen again.

"You can't bully me into this," I say. "You can't push your way to getting what you want. I'm doing the right thing for them, not you. It's no wonder Jolene left you, because you're selfish! God forbid you don't get your way. God forbid you have to think of anyone but yourself. God forbid you love. God forbid—"

Before I can say another word, Ian's lips are pressed against mine. I lock up completely. I don't breathe or move, in total shock. His hands are holding my face, refusing to let me get away. I couldn't if I wanted to because our lips are touching.

After a few seconds, Ian releases me. I stand there, unsure what the hell just happened. Ian kissed me. He just grabbed me and kissed me. I used to dream of his mouth on mine. So many nights I wished he would come to me, tell me he felt something, say he was sorry, kiss me again, love me, but he never did. Each day that passed my heart sank deeper into despair. Each week that went by I hardened myself to him. Each year it grew into a hate so deep we couldn't even be in the same room. But I've refused to let him see the damage he's done.

He just took that from me. With one touch of our lips, the pain returned with a vengeance. Without thinking, I lift my hand, and slap him across the face.

CHAPTER FOUR
ian

"What the fuck?" I scowl at London as if I can't understand why she hit me. The truth is, I know exactly why my cheek is stinging right now.

What I don't know is why I fucking kissed her in the first place. One second I was standing there listening to her go off about what a terrible person I am, listing all my faults and flaws, digging at me where it hurts the most, and the next second I had the uncontrollable impulse to crush my mouth against hers like I was nineteen again.

"What the fuck?" Her face is all fiery outrage. Her hands are clenched into fists. "You argue with me, you insult me, you take me down a notch in front the kids, and then out of nowhere you kiss me, and you have the nerve to ask me 'what the fuck?' I should be asking you that question, Ian! So what the fuck?"

"I didn't take you down a notch." I straighten my tie, although it was perfectly straight. "I was putting the kids first, like we're supposed to. It's obvious to me the kids don't want to live in a house that reminds them of their parents."

"And it's obvious to me you're just as self-centered as you ever were. Some things never change." Her icy green eyes narrow, and she jerks her chin at me. "Now why did you kiss me? I deserve an answer."

Since the whole truth isn't an option, I give her a partial one, retreating into the role of Insensitive Asshole, which is what she thinks I am anyway. "To shut you up."

Her jaw drops, and she puts a hand on her chest. "To shut me up? Did those words really just come out of your mouth? Because that's a new low even for you."

"It worked, didn't it?" I shrug. "Told you I'm a smart guy."

"You are unfuckingbelievable."

"You know, I believe I've heard that from a woman before. Of course, she was wearing much less clothing than you are . . ." Just to be an even bigger jerk, I drop my eyes from her face down to her black high heels and slowwwwly bring my gaze up again. "But I'm pretty sure those were her exact words."

She parks her hands on her hips. "See? This is exactly why you are not fit to raise those kids. I cannot imagine what your sister was thinking."

That pisses me off. "Maybe she was thinking that she knows what's best for her children—to be raised by a blood relative who loves them, who can give them every advantage, and who will teach them not to be condescending, judgmental assholes that think they know everything." A little harsh, maybe, but I'm sick and tired of her treating me like dog shit on the bottom of her shoe. Just because I don't reveal my feelings very often doesn't mean they don't exist.

She's taken aback, and for a second I think she might hit me again. I don't back away. Let her do it if she wants to.

But she doesn't. She drops her arms to her sides, gathers herself up and takes a deep breath. When she speaks, her voice is calm. "I am going to be the grown-up in the room and stop fighting with you. You want to move the kids into your house? Fine. You think they'll be happy to leave the only home they've ever known? Fine. You think your lifestyle is suitable for children? Fine."

"As a matter of fact, that's exactly what I think. So you can just turn around, and walk your little grown-up ass right on out of here." I gesture toward the door. "I don't need you to tell me how to raise my nieces and nephew. And I don't need your help."

She crosses her arms over her chest. "You don't think you need my help?" Her expression is almost amused, which pisses me off even more.

"No. I don't." I stand up a little taller. "You can see them whenever you want to, but I've changed my mind about sharing them. Sabrina and David left them to me. And the last thing I need is you in my face all the time, telling me I'm doing things wrong. They're my blood, my family, my responsibility."

Tossing her head back, she laughs. "I didn't even know you knew the meaning of that word. Good for you." She turns, grabs her purse from beneath the conference table, and heads for the door. I can't help but look at her ass, and I hate that it's fantastic. I don't want to want her like that. How many more fucking years will I have to fight it?

When she reaches the door, she looks over her shoulder at me. "In case you're wondering, I'll find another ride home. Oh, and make sure the kids buckle their seatbelts. I'd forgotten what a reckless driver you are."

She's gone before I can bite back.

Damn it.

I rub my face with both hands, feeling the days-old scruff against my palms. I need a shave. I need a haircut. I need a grip on my life.

I stare out the window without seeing anything as reality sinks in. Ten days ago I was on top of the world and loving every second of it. Rich. Single. Fearless. Old enough to know better, but young enough to do it anyway.

Now I'm a divorced "father" of three. Clueless. Sad. Scared.

Defeated, I sink into the chair at the head of the conference table and pinch the bridge of my nose. What am I going to do now? In the past when I needed advice, I went to my sister. I can't do that anymore.

My throat closes up, and I swallow hard, squeezing my eyes shut. "What were you thinking, Sab?" I whisper. "I wish you were here to tell me. I need you."

But the room stays silent except for the quiet whoosh of the central air conditioning and the tick of a clock on the wall.

Sabrina would argue with me, wouldn't she? She was always on my side unless London was involved. She'd tell me my ego was too big, my attitude was shitty, and my pride was getting in the way of moving forward. She'd be furious that I was being a dick to London, but goddammit, she deserved it. Calling me selfish, accusing me of being a bully, bringing up Jolene. London's hatred of me has nothing to do with Jolene and she knows it. She's just bitter about the past, as if there's anything I can do about it now. She doesn't even know why I did what I did, and she has no idea I did it for her. She should thank me. But no—to do that would mean listening to my side, and she's made it perfectly clear she's not the least bit interested in that.

I wish I hadn't kissed her just now. All it did was stir up feelings in me that were better left buried in the past.

"Ian?"

Startled, I jump up from the chair to see my mother coming through the door of the conference room. Her eyes are red and puffy, her complexion ashen, and she looks older than her sixty-six years.

"Yeah?" My voice is scratchy.

"Daddy and I are leaving. We're going to take the kids back to their house so they can pack up some things. Chris says they're moving in with you?" She studies me carefully, and I feel as if all the cracks in my armor are showing.

I clear my throat and speak firmly. "Yes. My house is bigger, they love the pool, and . . . London will be close by."

My mother tilts her head. "I hear you told her you didn't need her help."

Fucking London! "Maybe I don't need her help," I say defensively, running a hand through my hair. "Maybe I can handle them on my own. Sabrina seemed to think so."

She crosses her arms. "Ian. Being a parent is hard enough when there are two of them in the house. Being a single parent is even tougher, and you have your hands full. Chris is trying to keep it together for the girls, but he's struggling. Morgan is a mess—she hasn't stopped crying, barely comes out of her room, and hardly eats. And did you notice that Ruby has stopped talking?"

"What?"

"She won't talk. Not at all to me or Daddy, scarcely a word to Chris and Morgan." She glances over her shoulder out the door. "But I just heard her telling London she didn't want her to go."

A vise closes around my heart.

"You're going to need her help," my mother says, slowly and firmly. "You should apologize."

No fucking way. "Apologize! For what?"

"For whatever it is you said to her. She tried to hide it, but she was in tears when she walked out of here, and it was clearly because of you." My mother sniffled, and touched at her eyes with a white handkerchief. "I don't understand why you two can't get along. She was Sabrina's best friend. Practically family. Why can't you be civil to each other?"

"I don't know," I lied.

"Well, you'd better figure it out. Those kids are going to need both of you." Her voice softens and her eyes fill again. "Your sister trusted you, Ian. Don't let her down."

"Jesus, Mom. Enough." Overwhelmed by guilt and grief and fear and the feeling that the ground is giving way under my feet, I walk to the door and shoulder past her before she can make me feel worse.

∼

On my way home, I call Drea. "Hey," I say when she picks up her cell. "I can't come in tonight."

She groans. "I'm sorry, I know I shouldn't give you shit today of all days, but you said you could be there."

"I thought I could. Look, it's a Wednesday night. We won't be that busy."

"That's what you said last time you didn't come in on a weekday night, and there were two fights in line."

I frown and change lanes without signaling. You're a reckless driver, I hear in my head. "You'll have to handle it, Drea. I've got family issues."

She sighs. "Okay. I'll see if I can get a second bouncer for the door tonight. Maybe another one for inside, too."

"Fine."

A pause. "The service was beautiful."

"Thanks."

"Are you . . . okay?"

"I'm fine. Call me if there's an emergency." I end the call before she can even reply.

I'm not okay. I'm so far from okay I can't even see where the line for okay begins. I'm livid, hurt, confused, and if I'm honest, I'm scared out of my fucking mind. Three kids. I am now responsible for three kids. And I have to be good at it, because that's what my sister wanted.

It will be a huge lifestyle change for me, but for those kids, I'll do it.

What I won't do is pretend I'm not very upset at said sister. First, she goes and dies on me--I know that's not the most mature way to look at it, but I'm a broken man. Then, she leaves everyone under the fucking sun a goodbye letter except me. Why?

Of all the people who needed one, I needed it the most.

London gets one.

The kids, of course, get one.

Hell, even our parents, who we only see at Christmas, get one.

But not her brother, the one she decided should be in charge of raising her kids. Nope. I'm just the low man on the totem pole.

When I get home, I go upstairs and look into all the bedrooms. Needless to say, they are not suitable for children. One has a free-standing sex swing in the corner, which I hurriedly disassemble and hide in the loft of my three-car garage. One has a collection of toys under the bed—and I'm not talking about the kind from Fisher Price. I gather them all up and stuff them into a suitcase, then shove the suitcase in the attic. The last one might be okay except there's a mirror on the ceiling. I cringe. How the fuck am I going to explain that? I only have three spare rooms, so if the girls don't want to share, one of the kids will end up in here. There's no time to remove it, so I decide to move the damn bed and claim it was here when I moved in.

My very discreet housekeeper changes the bedding any time I have guests, and she always keeps the rooms clean and the bathrooms stocked with fresh towels, but I double-check it all anyway. I want to feel as prepared as possible.

Downstairs, I look around at my kitchen and living room. What else would the kids need besides a place to sleep and put their clothes?

Food?

Shit. That could be a problem. My housekeeper grocery shops for me, but I'm not much of a cook.

I walk over to my fridge and open it. A bunch of takeout boxes. Eggs. Bacon. A few apples. Ketchup and mustard. In the freezer are a few bottles of booze, trays of ice cubes, a frozen pizza, some chicken breasts, and a mystery container, probably full of something Sabrina made and brought me, but has been in here so long I forgot about it. I take out the pizza box and stare at it, but it's not enough to feed four people. Six if my parents come. Seven if I break down and include London.

Sticking the box back in the freezer, I walk over to the sliding glass door that leads out to the pool and look across the back yard. She's outside—I can see her standing on her deck, holding a glass of wine in one hand. She's changed out of the black suit into a tank top and shorts, and her hair is down.

When I bought this house two years ago, I had no idea the yard backed up to hers. When Sabrina realized it and told me, I had a good laugh about how furious it was going to make London to live so close to me. To be unable to ignore my existence like she'd been so hell-bent on doing for the previous fifteen years. To be forced to see and hear me enjoying life while she's over there drinking wine and talking to her cat.

She turns in my direction, but I know she can't see me. My windows are mirrored glass, so I can see out, but you can't even see a shadow from the other side. I like my privacy. She takes a sip from her glass, and I think how easy it would be for me to walk out there and call to her. Invite her over. Tell her I could use a drink too. Tell her I'm sorry—I didn't mean to be such a dick today, but my best friend is gone and my life is upside down and I don't want anyone to know I feel so fucking alone I could cry.

But she'd only say *I told you so*. That's what women do. You show them any sign of weakness and they fucking move in for the kill. Those moments today when she pretended she wanted to get along with me so we could give the kids hope were just bullshit. She only wanted to use this as another opportunity to prove I'm an irresponsible jackass, unfit to take care of the kids. One more *fuck you for what you did to me, Ian*, as if I haven't already paid the price.

After giving her one last glare, I move away from the window, pick up my phone off the counter, and call my mom to find out what time she'll be over with the kids and what they like on their pizza.

∼

"I don't want to watch Captain America, Chris," Morgan says as she rips the remote from his hand. "I want to watch Gilmore Girls. You don't get to hog the remote!"

"Well, you're not the boss!" He grabs it back. "I'm older, so I get to decide. Brat!"

My fucking head is going to explode. All they do is fight. How the hell did Sabrina not blow her eardrums out? Listening to these two is giving me a migraine. Either I've blocked out this part of my childhood or Sabrina and I got along better.

It's been an hour since my parents left. They ate pizza with us, kissed the kids, smiled at me, and that was it. Tomorrow they head back to Florida. My father has some kind of meeting and since I told them I didn't need their help, they're going. I'm a goddamn fool.

I'm not going to survive one night from the looks of it.

My perfect house is a mess. Shit all over the place from the kids tossing their crap. This isn't even half of their stuff, either. This was just a bag each of clothes and their must-haves. The rest comes with the movers.

Mom planned to go through the house, sell or get rid of anything we didn't need, but since I assured her she didn't have to stick around because I'm a man and could handle it, I'm fucked.

"You're so stupid!"

"And you're a bitch!" Chris yells.

That's it.

"Guys, guys!" I walk into what was once my very quiet family room and stand in front of the television. "You." I point to Chris. "Don't you ever call her a bitch or you won't like what happens." Then I turn to Morgan. "And you, don't call him stupid."

"Sorry, Uncle Ian," Chris says.

"Yeah," Morgan sighs. "Sorry."

Now I feel like an asshole. I've never wanted to be a disciplinarian, but shit, I have to be now. "There are more than ten places to watch a movie in this house. Why don't you go downstairs, and you go up to your room, and I'll take back this one?"

"I don't like being upstairs alone," Morgan admits.

"And you have a bigger screen up here," Chris says with a shrug.

Typical man. "No shit, that's why I watch the games in here." I smirk and point for them to vacate. "Go. Figure it out."

They get to their feet, both grumbling under their breath, and I stand tall as they leave the room.

There. I did it. I parented or adulted or some shit. Look at me being all grown up and whatnot. My eyes dart out to the back, to where London would be.

Take that! I can do this without your damn help! I mentally yell at her, like the mature adult I am while pointing my finger and puffing out my chest.

"Uncle Ian," Morgan says as I'm posturing at the window, thankful that London definitely can't see in.

I spin around. "What's up? I thought you went upstairs."

"What are you doing?" she asks, trying to hold back her laugh.

"I'm... looking out the window."

"Right. Is Aunt London out on the deck?"

"I don't know."

She peers around me. "Can't you see?"

I glare at who was once my favorite niece. "I wasn't looking for her."

"Uh huh." Morgan snorts. "Do you like her or something?"

What is with the twenty questions? I cross my arms over my chest. "Do you like rabid animals?"

She tilts her head. "Umm, no. Does anyone?"

"Then there's your answer. I like to think of her as a raccoon you need to stay ten feet away from because she'll bite you in the ass."

"Whatever," Morgan says as she rolls her eyes. "Look, Ruby won't come out of her room."

"Still?" I ask.

Of all the people in the world the kid will talk to, why does it have to be London?

"I'll go try," I say. I was just the big man of the house a few minutes ago, and I'm going to do it again. I own today, and these kids need to see who is boss.

This guy.

I march upstairs to the guest room where I put Ruby.

"Ruby." I call her name. When she doesn't come to the door, I open it. She sits up on the bed, and her big blue eyes meet mine. "Do you want to eat?" I ask.

She shakes her head.

"Are you thirsty?" I go for another question.

Again with the head shake.

"Do you want to watch a movie?" I ask, praying it's anything but that damn purple dinosaur. I swear, Morgan made me sit through hours of that when she was a kid, and I never wished for a meteor to hit Earth more than I did at that time. I would've done anything to put myself out of my misery, but she cried the second the DVD ended, until I started it again.

Ruby nods.

At least we're getting somewhere now.

"Okay, well, you have to tell me what you want to watch."

I decide this time I'm not giving her a yes or no question. Maybe I can get her to talk by not giving an option.

Ruby hops out of bed, takes my hand, and leads me down to where all the movies are.

"Ruby, you have to tell me," I try again. "I need you to talk instead of show me."

Her lip starts to tremble and tears form.

Fuck.

"No, no, no, don't cry. It's okay." I pat her shoulders. "Ruby, you don't have to talk, just show Uncle Ian what you want."

I see it coming like a tidal wave. I can't stop it. I can't do anything to prepare for it because there isn't time.

The tears fall down her cheeks and a sobbing sound escapes this tiny person.

Holy fucking hell, she has a set of pipes.

The sound is a mix of a siren and some kind of animal in

excruciating pain. I look to Morgan who stands there, shell-shocked. "Morgan! What do I do?" I yell to her.

"I don't know!" she replies.

Helpful.

I get down on my knees in front of my weeping little niece. "Ruby, baby, don't cry. I'm right here." I try to gather her in my arms, thinking I've seen parents do this—they offer comfort by embracing them.

Another wail comes out as soon as I touch her, piercing the room. I wince and go for another tactic.

"Okay." I move away from her. "No touching, got it. If you want to cry, that's fine. I get it. Crying is helpful, right?"

Ruby's tears slice through me. I don't know what to do. I look up to the sky, wondering what my sister was thinking. I'm completely fucking lost here.

I get to my feet, but as soon as I move away, she screams out again, and my black heart breaks. "I don't know what to do here, sweetheart," I admit to her. "Do you want me to hug you or go away? Do you want a cookie? Ice cream? Maybe a doll? We can go to the store!"

"I don't think you're supposed to give her things." Morgan shakes her head at me.

"Do you have a better idea?"

She rolls her eyes, and Ruby goes on and on.

Morgan looks down at her nails and then back up to me. "I know someone who could help."

CHAPTER FIVE
London

U gh! I hate that man.
I hate him.
I hate that I want to hate him more than I already do.
I grab the bottle of pinot and pour another glass. Stupid asshole. Calling me lonely. Telling me I'm condescending and judgmental. Ha! I'm only those things because I see the truth about him and he doesn't like it.
God forbid I not be one of his little groupies who tell him what he wants to hear. I know what he is—a user.
I wander over to the sliding door leading to my deck. "And good luck keeping those kids from me!" I yell at his house, lifting my middle finger in the air, hoping he can see through the glass. "Prick!"
We'll see what happens the first time he needs help. I'll sit here in all my judgy-ness and tell him to figure it out his damn self.
I hope his balls fall off.
That would really teach him.
Refusing to look in his direction one more second, I march into my living room and sink onto the couch. I lean my head back,

allowing the almost-finished glass of wine to warm my extremities.

I turn my head to the side, seeing the unopened letter from Sabrina sticking out of my purse. She left six letters with her lawyer. One each for me, Chris, Morgan, and Ruby; one for her parents; and one for David's parents. The only person without a letter was Ian. Which of course spurred another outburst from him.

My heart begins to race and I instantly feel sick to my stomach. Can I really read it? Am I ever going to feel ready? Probably not. However, I miss her. I want to hear anything she has to say.

Leaning over, I take it in my hand, loving the scripted letters of my name in her handwriting. I slide my finger under the seal, slowly opening the flap. The sound of the paper opening causes my chest to tighten. I'm not sure how I'll get through this. I pull the letter out, decide to down my third glass of wine, tuck my feet under my butt, and read her last words to me.

London,

My best friend. My soul sister. The girl who has been through it all with me and never stopped loving me. This letter is so hard to write, but I had to do it. I remember Dad telling me about how no one should ever wonder what you felt after you were gone, so here I am. I've had a few glasses of wine so I could actually get through this version of hell. I hope you've had some too!

First, thank you. You're the best friend every girl should have. You've never judged me for the stupid things I've done, you loved me when I didn't listen to you, and you always had my back. We've been through so much, and I wouldn't have wanted any other friend beside me. I love you with my whole heart.

Second, you're probably a little mad at me right now. Don't be. Please understand we didn't make this decision lightly regarding the kids. We went back and forth a hundred times, but he's my brother, Lon. He's their uncle, and I know without a shadow of a doubt that you'll be there for them no matter what. I know that you'll love them, make sure he doesn't teach them bad habits, and you'll give them the woman's touch they'll need.

(Side note: this the most morbid shit I've ever had to do.)

Okay, back to pouring my heart out and pouring another glass of wine.

You and Ian may not get along, but please try. He's going to be stubborn, but then again, so will you. Just dig your heels in on being there for them. Chris will get bad advice from him--you'll need to make sure he doesn't take it. Morgan will probably drive him crazy, you can allow that. Ruby will get away with anything because ... have you seen her eyes? That girl already knows how to work the system.

I'm hoping that this letter never makes it to you. I want to tell you in person what your friendship means to me. Just know that even if I'm gone, I'll miss you so much.

Lastly, I'm going to say this because I'm gone and you can't kill me . . . forgive my damn brother already. Yes, he broke your heart, but if you didn't still have feelings for him, you wouldn't care so much.

He cares too. I know he does.

Love,

Sabrina

Tears slide down my face and I use the back of my hand to clear them away. Clutching the letter to my chest, I know I'll treasure this always, even if the ending was complete crazy talk.

I close my eyes, letting my emotions settle around me, both thankful I got to read that and wishing I never had to. The doorbell rings, and my head flops to the side. Who the hell could be here now?

The wine hits me when I stand, but I manage to get to the door without incident. When I open it, the door hits the rug, getting stuck, and I stumble backwards. Onto my ass. In front of the biggest ass I know.

"Are you drunk?" Ian asks.

I'm sure getting close to it.

"No, thanks for asking. I was just ... I'm fine."

I'm not telling him I just read the letter. The last thing I need is him asking me questions. If Sabrina wanted him to have one, she'd have written something to him. Plus, I'm not forgiving him anytime soon. He has to earn that.

"Great," he mumbles as he enters my house. "You're freaking toasted. Here." His hand is in front of me, but I don't need his help.

"God only knows where your hands have been," I sneer. Instead of doing what any sane person would, I roll to my stomach and get onto my hands and knees. "I'd rather crawl."

"Nice panties." Ian smirks.

This is why Sabrina was wrong. He's a total ass. I look at him from over my shoulder and glare. "I'm going commando."

"Hard to wear underwear with the stick up your ass, huh?"

When I get to the stairs, I manage to get myself upright without needing his stupid help, and lean against the railing. "Wouldn't you like to know?"

He shakes his head and moves closer. "I need your help."

I laugh right in his face. "That took less time than I thought."

Ian runs his hand down his face and mutters under his breath. "Did you think it was easy to say that?"

"Do you think I care?"

"This isn't about me or you. Ruby is screaming and you're the only one she'll talk to. I don't know what to do. She's hysterical and it's been ten minutes of the three of us trying to calm her. I know you hate me, and believe me, I fucking hate you too." He grits his teeth. "I'm asking you to help my niece—your niece."

As much as I hate to do anything for him, there's no way I can say no. Ruby is the sweetest thing in the world. I close my eyes, pull in a shaky breath, and do my best to sober up.

I look at Ian and see the stress in his face. "I'm not doing it for you."

He shrugs. "I didn't think you would."

As long as we're both clear.

"Let me chug some coffee," I say.

He rolls his eyes but doesn't refute me.

After I've drunk a cup of strong coffee and eaten some bread, I walk out the door. It's funny how quickly some things can sober you up. I remember being a little sloshed at a party, enjoying myself after graduation, and the minute Ian showed up with his slut girlfriend from college, my fun night was over.

"You know, you're a real buzz kill," I say as we're climbing down the stairs to the cut through our yards.

"What?"

"You always ruin my alcohol buzz," I reply.

He shakes his head and keeps moving.

I can hear Ruby crying as soon as we get past my deck. "Did you try talking to her?" I ask.

Ian stops walking suddenly and I plow into the back of him. He turns, grabbing my arm, and pulls me to his chest. The smell of his cologne, the feel of his skin on mine, causes my heart to race. I hate my weak body for being drawn to him, but my drunken mind can't stop the thoughts of what it felt like to have his lips on mine.

I've replayed that kiss a million times already, the way his hands scrunched my shirt in the back, how he was demanding with his tongue, and then there was his taste. Why does he have to be so fucking hot?

"I'm not a fucking idiot. Of course I tried talking to her."

I shake my head, getting rid of the thoughts of him touching me, and put my armor back in place. "I had to ask."

"Be more careful where you walk," he says, and then releases me.

Of course he doesn't think about me that way. I'm simple, ugly, plain, and a bitch in his world. He doesn't see me as a woman, he never has.

Traitorous body wanting a man who only cares for himself.

It takes a few more seconds before we're in the house, and Ruby is beside herself. The tears stream, her cries are loud, and she's worked herself up pretty good. "Ruby, honey, come here." I squat down and she comes running to my arms. "There, there."

I hold her against my body as she cries. The screaming slows, but she's a mess.

"How the—?" Ian says looking at Ruby in my arms.

"She's scared," I explain. This little girl has had her entire world flipped upside down. I have no idea why I'm the only person she'll come to right now, but that's not my worry—Ruby is.

Ian sits on the floor beside me, his hand reaching out, tucking the strand of blond hair behind her ear. "I'm here for you, princess. Uncle Ian loves you and just wants you to smile. That's all."

Ruby's little arms tighten. "Milk?" she asks.

"You want some milk?" I repeat.

She nods.

"Can I get you some milk?" Ian tries again.

She glares at him. "Aunt London."

This poor kid. And since I refuse to move in with Ian to be his daily translator, I have to find a way to make this better. I rub Ruby's back and think. "Ruby," I say softly. "If you want Auntie London to get your milk, then I need you to help me, can you do that?"

She smiles.

"I need you to sit on Uncle Ian's lap," I explain. Her tiny body goes stiff. "I'm not going anywhere but to the kitchen. You'll be able to see me the whole time. Okay?"

Ian watches me, and instead of the normal hatred in his eyes, I see appreciation. I know coming to me for help couldn't have been easy for him. I don't know that I would've gone to him if the tables were turned, but his love for Ruby overshadowed his own desires.

I gently lift Ruby, and her arms start to slide from around my neck as I transfer her into his lap. Ian doesn't move or say a word, he allows me to control the situation, which is totally unlike him.

Ruby rests her head on Ian's chest, and I sit there for second. Both of us watching each other. Both of us saying so much in a simple look. Both of us lost.

I catch myself before I let my heart soften too much. Ian is the kind of guy who takes advantage of people's vulnerability—or at least mine.

I get to my feet and go into the kitchen. Opening the fridge, I look around for a carton of milk but don't see one. "Ian," I call out. "Where's the milk?"

"Isn't there some in there?"

"Not that I can see."

He stands and takes Ruby by the hand, leading her over to one of the stools at the kitchen island. "Wait right here, baby. Uncle Ian is going to get you some milk."

"I don't know how, unless you've got a cow in your garage."

He barely looks at me as he elbows me aside and opens the fridge wider, leaning down so he can see inside. "Hmm. Maybe I don't have any milk."

"Then why would you offer it to her?" I toss a hand in the air.

"I thought there might be some in here, okay?" He shuts the fridge and glares at me as he makes excuses. "My housekeeper does the shopping for me. I don't even eat dairy, so I wasn't sure if she'd bought milk this week or not."

I roll my eyes. "Well, maybe you should put it on your housekeeper's list, now that you are a responsible parent and all." I use little air quotes around the words just to get deeper under his skin.

He looks like he wants to spit nails at me, but he goes over to the counter where a little pad of paper and pen sit next to two open boxes of pizza. Both pies are half-eaten and need to be put away.

Ian grabs the pen. "Milk," he says, shooting me a dirty look as he writes it down. Then he looks over at Ruby and softens his tone. "What else would you like from the grocery store, sweetheart? I'll run out right now."

"I can go to the store," I offer.

Another dirty look. "You've been drinking. You're not going anywhere." He turns back to Ruby. "You didn't eat any pizza, honey. Would you like something else for dinner?"

Ruby shakes her head and starts to weep again, her little shoulders trembling.

Immediately I go embrace her, tucking her head beneath my chin, rocking her gently. "You know what? I have milk at my house, sweetie. I'll go get it for you. I even have the chocolate syrup you like."

"I'll go get the milk from your house." Ian practically vaults over the kitchen counter in an attempt to beat me to the back door, and I quicken my pace. We reach it at the same time and he stands with his back to it, blocking me from getting out. "You stay here with them."

"Don't tell me what to do," I snarl between clenched teeth, trying to push him aside. "And get out of my way, you big bully."

"No." He doesn't budge an inch. In the hours since the service, he's changed from his dark suit into jeans and a T-shirt so fitted I can see his six-pack rippling beneath it.

Show-off.

"This is something I can do, so I'm going to do it," he declares, glancing at Ruby and lowering his voice. "She won't even talk to me."

"Maybe if she didn't see you being such a jerk to me, she wouldn't be scared of you," I whisper fiercely. "You want her to trust you, you have to show her you're not going to hurt her."

He's insulted. "These kids know I would never hurt them."

"No, they don't. Everything they thought they knew, every reason they had to feel safe, is gone. They're lost and sad and scared, even if they don't show it." I look at Chris and Morgan on the couch. "Or show it in different ways. Now move."

"No." He turns around, putting his back to me and his hand on the door handle, keeping it shut.

I wrap my hands around his waist and try to move him, but

it's like trying to budge a Giant Sequoia. Next, I grab his muscular forearm, trying to pry his hand off the door handle. His skin is warm beneath my palms, and hell if it doesn't turn me on to touch him. What is wrong with me? "Damn you, Ian," I say quietly. "You came to me, remember?'

Our eyes meet over his shoulder, and the line between desire and contempt grows even thinner. He looks at my lips and then down at my hands on him. "I remember a lot of things. Now I'm going to your house to get the milk, and if you know what's good for you, you'll stay here with the kids. Understand?"

I don't know if it's the alcohol or his words that have my head spinning and my blood rushing to all manner of inappropriate places. What does he mean by a lot of things? Surprise makes me loosen my grip, and he takes advantage of it, shrugging me off, opening the door, and stomping into the yard. For a second, I just stand there watching him disappear into the dark, my heart pumping hard inside my chest. Let him go, I tell myself. He needs to cool off. You need to cool off. I slide the door closed.

But a split-second later, I find myself turning toward the kids. "Christopher, I'll be right back, okay?"

"Okay."

Because I'm too wound up—and wined up—to let this go. He can't play with me like this. Not after what he did back then. And not after kissing me like that today.

He has a good enough head start that he's already letting himself into my kitchen through the sliding door off my deck by the time I catch up. "Hey," I say breathlessly, ramming the door shut behind me. "I didn't say you could come into my house."

"I didn't ask your permission." He marches over to the fridge and opens it, the interior light spilling onto him like a spotlight on a darkened stage. From where I stand, I see him in profile, and my stomach flips at the cut of his jaw, the stubborn set of his mouth, the tightness of the sleeve around his bicep. I'm sixteen again, watching him and wishing he would look at me differently. Then I'm seventeen, working up the courage to flirt with him, ecstatic when he steals a kiss at a party. Then I'm eighteen, all my dreams coming true in one perfect night, and I offer him the one gift I can never get back.

And he took it. He made promises. He made me believe we were going to be together. I was ready to give up everything I had worked so hard for to be with him. Turns out, I was just another notch on his bedpost.

So why did he kiss me today?

Why is there still this spark between us?

How is it possible to hate someone and still want his hands on you?

I need answers.

Frustrated and confused, I march over to where he stands and get between him and the refrigerator, pushing the door shut and leaning back against it. "Tell me why you really kissed me today."

"I told you. To shut you up."

"That's the only reason?" I can feel the heat coming off him, and it's not all anger.

Ian takes me by the shoulders, pinning me back against the cold stainless steel. "Now you listen to me. I've had about all I can take of your smug, sanctimonious behavior today. Stop it."

"Or else what?" I challenge, full of heat and liquid courage.

He leans toward me menacingly. "Or else you're not going to like the consequences."

I lift my chin. "Try me."

With a grunt of frustration, he crushes his lips to mine just like he did in the conference room today, only this time I kiss him back. His hand slides around the back of my neck and into my hair, his fingers curling into a fist. I gasp at the sharp sting on my scalp, and he takes advantage of my open mouth, his tongue stroking inside it.

I reach beneath his shirt and run my hands up his rippling abs and sculpted chest. His bare skin is hot and smooth under my palms. His mouth travels down one side of my throat, his tongue warm and wet. He pulls me away from the fridge, slips his hands beneath my thighs and lifts me up so that my legs are wrapped around his waist.

Inside my head is a dizzying refrain. *He wants me, he wants me, he wants me.*

The mental victory feels as good as his body against mine. I take his face in my hands, his scruffy jaw rough against my fingers, and our mouths coming together again. He turns and sets me on the kitchen counter and the kiss grows deeper and more feverish, until all of a sudden he grabs me by the wrists, forcing my hands off him.

"Enough," he says, breathing hard. "Enough. You drive me fucking crazy, London. And I don't know what kind of games you're playing tonight, but I'm not interested."

And just like that, my self-esteem is crushed by his callousness—again.

"You're one to talk about games," I snap, yanking my arms from his grip. "How about the way you played me in the past?"

He steps back, runs a hand through his hair. "Jesus, that was almost twenty fucking years ago. We were kids."

"So what? I believed everything you said that night. I gave you my virginity. And it was all just a lark for you!"

"No, it wasn't."

"What else was I supposed to think? One night you say you're all mine, the next night you were with somebody else. I saw you, remember?"

He says nothing. Doesn't move a muscle.

"You never even said you were sorry," I inform him.

He points at me. "You think you're so smart. You think you know everything. Well, you don't."

"I know I should have stayed away from you."

"That, sweetheart, is a lesson we've both learned." Turning away from me, he opens the fridge and stares into it. The milk is right there in front of his face, but apparently he can't see it.

Sliding off the counter, I shoulder him aside and grab the

plastic half-gallon of skim myself. Then I shut the door and slam the milk onto the counter like a gavel. "Here. Take it."

Expecting him to leave now that he has what he wants, I'm surprised when he keeps standing there.

"What?" I ask flatly. "Surely you don't need my help pouring a glass of milk. You want to play the hero, Ian, go play him. I know how you love the role."

He grasps the handle of the half-gallon, but he doesn't pick it up. "She's going to want you."

I cross my arms over my chest. "And?"

"And . . ." He doesn't look at me as he considers his words. "And I think you should come back to the house."

God, he was so damn stubborn. Why couldn't he just admit that he needed me as much as the kids did? Why couldn't he be straight with me for once, and not give me that cocky asshole façade? Why couldn't he see that all I wanted was a little fucking sincerity from him? I shake my head. "Not good enough."

He glares at me. "Fuck you." Then he swings the milk off the counter and storms out the back door, slamming it behind him.

CHAPTER SIX
London

I must've lost my freaking mind.

That's the only explanation I can come up with for what just happened. I might have some sort of disease that destroys common sense and logic. Nothing else makes sense as to why I kissed him like that, let him kiss me, and somehow expected something other than exactly what I got. I'm still standing alone in my kitchen trying to process everything that just happened when I hear three loud knuckle-raps on the glass.

I freeze, take a deep breath, and head to the door. It's him, of course. "So you knock now?"

His jaw is tight. "Please come back to the house."

"Why should I?"

Exhaling loudly, he tries again. "I need you. They need you."

I need him to say it. It's stupid and doesn't change anything between us, but it has to be because I'm worth something more.

"Are you asking me for help because you need a babysitter while you're out at the club?"

Please, say no. Please tell me it's because you care, even just a little for me.

He shrugs. "Partly."

I try to shut the door in his face but he stops it with the heel of his hand. Instead of Neanderthalling his way into the house, he just stands there.

"I can't do this with you," I admit. "I can't. You want just one thing, and screw anyone else's needs in the meantime."

"You think I want this . . . that I'm enjoying myself having to ask you for help now?"

"I don't know what you want, I don't think *you* know what you want!"

He runs his hand over his face. "Well, excuse me! But I wasn't the one pushing your restraint right there." He points to the fridge. "That was all you, sweetheart. You're just as guilty for what happened. I know you like me to be the bad guy, but fuck, London. You initiated it this time. So don't play your 'I'm so perfect and Ian is the devil' shit on me." His voice rises as he mimics me.

Asshole.

"Fuck off."

He's right, though. It was me this time. I wanted . . . no, I needed him. I needed to feel something—anything—to know that it was me he wanted and not some bullshit excuse about keeping me quiet. I need to know why I still feel something for him.

And if I'm honest, it's the most alive I've felt in a long time. Ian is the gasoline and I'm the match—when we connect, we could start a forest fire.

"Right, fuck off," Ian scoffs. "I kiss you and you slap me. You push me to do it again so you can what? Get answers to something that happened a million years ago?"

He doesn't get it. I was doing just fine before he kissed me today. For decades, I've been able to go without a single touch from him and be just fine. Then the moment in the office happened and I've lost my ever-loving mind.

"You confused me with that kiss. I'm so tired of you using me, confusing me, and then brushing me off like I don't matter!"

The air between us crackles. "I brush you off? Are you kidding me?"

I move closer toward him. "No, I'm not kidding you, Ian. I want to put this all behind us for once. So let's have it out. Let's get all the dirty laundry out in the open so I can move the hell on."

"We're not going down this road. Not today. Not ever. Fuck! How are you the only female on this planet that can make me this fucking crazy?" Ian yells the last part. "Why, when my entire life feels like it's falling apart, am I standing here, wishing I could shut you up again with my mouth? Why, when I'm so far past the point of angry, all I want to do is . . ." He stops, and my breath hitches.

I wait for him to continue, both of us standing here, staring at each other. My heart races as I wait for the words to come from his lips. To tell me something real. Tell me I'm not alone.

But instead, Ian retreats, like always. He shakes his head with his eyes closed, and my heart breaks. "Don't worry, this won't happen again. We both know it was a mistake and I don't need any more reasons for you to hate me. I think you've stockpiled enough already."

"I don't really hate you," I admit.

His head jerks back and he closes his eyes. "What the hell is it about you? Why do we do this to each other?"

"I don't know." If he's not going to admit his feelings, I damn sure won't admit mine. "Whatever. You've already said it was a mistake."

Or that I'm the mistake. Either one applies.

Fool me once, shame on you. Fool me twice, shame on me.

I release a heavy breath. "I'm tired of this."

"Of what exactly?"

Caring about you so much but pretending to hate you more.

"Thinking things could ever change."

I'm done with him and feeling this way. I'll be there for those kids because I love them with my whole heart. No matter what lingering issues are between Ian and me, we're not entering any kind of relationship different from what it's been for years.

Hostility and resentment.

Because hate is easier than love. If I hate him and he lets me down, I'm not left disappointed.

Ian sighs. He looks up to the sky and then back to me. "I know, I'm an asshole. You're better than me, and I'm never going to change and you'll always hate me. Let's chalk this up to grief and your inability to hold your liquor."

My walls are back up and the door we opened just now is cemented shut. "Prick."

"I got a big one of those, huh?"

Yeah, you do.

"I've had bigger," I lie.

No need to inflate his already ridiculous ego.

"Whatever you say, London. Now will you please come back with me and help? I'm sorry I disturbed your very busy night with your new friends Pinot and Chardonnay."

"Sure, only because you'll pay for this later." I smile, ignoring the jab.

He groans as I saunter past him and his voice is low, but I hear him clearly. "I don't doubt that."

The truth is, as pissed off as I was, I would've gone after him. Not just because of the kids, but because Ian is the weak link in my iron chain. Sabrina used to laugh because no matter how much I "hated" him, if he needed help, I would still help—with an attitude, of course. And I could never let Ruby suffer—she's too sweet to deserve that. I just wanted to calm myself down before having to face him.

We walk back to his house and as we get to his pool deck, he grabs my arm.

"I need to say something." He clears his throat. "Whatever you think that was back there on my part, you're probably wrong. You have a long history of thinking the worst of me—"

"I'm not—"

His hand covers my mouth. "Shut up for once and listen," Ian commands. "I've let you go on thinking whatever you want because if that's what you believe, nothing I say will change your mind. But hear this." His hand drops. "I'm sorry. This isn't how I want things to be with us."

I have no idea what he's apologizing for. For what happened before? Walking out and breaking my eighteen-year-old heart? Being a jerk today?

"What exactly are you sorry for?" I ask, my voice shaky.

"Everything. I know you're suffering the loss of your best friend, like I am, and we're acting like idiots," Ian admits. "I never should've said the things I did. Take your pick of the shit I've done and apply it."

"I'm sorry, too," I say, looking down at the ground. "We've both been acting—poorly. And I don't hate you. I wish I hated you. It would make things easier, it would mean I don't care."

He looks to the sky and laughs. "She'd both love and hate this, you know?"

I don't have to ask who he's talking about. "She would. She'd say that what just happened was long overdue. She'd tell us we were being stupid, and then she'd tell me never to speak of it again—unlike any other time I've told her about a kiss," I smile thinking of Sabrina. "Although, if she were alive, we never would've kissed."

She had no problems telling me the reason I hated Ian so much was because I really loved him. The thing about love is that it's irrational and stupid. I work with statistics and analyze hard data—I weigh probabilities and risks, and think in truths and facts.

Truth—Ian broke my heart.

Truth—Ian is the man I've never gotten over.

Fact—Ian is a selfish player who doesn't give a shit about me.

Fact—I want to rip his clothes off and fuck his brains out.

Those four things combined equals a disastrous outcome. But my best friend was a romantic at heart. She believed love conquered everything. She was a fool when it came to that line of thinking.

Ian raises his chin. "Or maybe it was bound to happen. Maybe we've been fighting it for so long we finally snapped. Maybe I've wanted to kiss you for—"

"Oh my God!" Morgan's voice breaks the moment. "You guys kissed?"

"Great," Ian groans.

"I knew it! I knew you liked her! Is that what took you guys so long? I was coming to find you because Chris thought maybe you got lost, but instead you were kissing. Are you guys like, together now?"

Oh, to be twelve again. However, I don't miss the key thing she said. "You like me?"

Morgan snorts. "Of course he does. You know how stupid boys are. They're only mean to girls they like. Since you guys can't seem to be nice to each other at all, it's obvious."

"Go inside before I ground you or whatever it is adults do," Ian instructs her.

"Telling the truth is always best, Uncle Ian," Morgan tosses back at him.

"The women in my life are going to drive me to drink," he says as the screen door shuts. "It's no wonder men die first. We can't wait to get away from you all!"

I laugh. "Yeah, because men are such a treat."

"I am. I can't speak for anyone else," Ian says as we walk in.

"Right."

When we get in the house the sight before me brings tears to my eyes. Christopher is asleep with Ruby on his chest. She has her thumb in her mouth, and is passed out. He looks like his father right now. Ruby's other hand is gripping his shirt, holding on to her brother.

"Should we move her?" I ask.

He nods. "I'll put her to bed."

Ian lifts her effortlessly into his arms, and she stirs a little, but settles. Chris sits up straight. "It's okay, honey," I whisper. "Why don't you head up and get some sleep?"

Chris gets up, shuffling his feet. I head into the kitchen and clean up a bit, as well as start a list of . . . well, real food.

I open the fridge again and then compose the list.

Milk

Fruit

Vegetables

Juice

Cheese

Just buy the damn store since you have nothing.

How the hell does he function? Seriously, there's nothing here that's actually edible. I give up on the list and head upstairs to check on the kids. Morgan is in her room, her earbuds in, as she lies on the bed. I knock softly on the open door, and she sits up.

"Hey," I say as I enter. "You doing okay?"

She shrugs. "I'm not sure."

"I get that." I move to her bed and sit beside her. "Want to talk about it?"

"Not much to say. My mom and dad are dead. I'm living in Uncle Ian's funhouse, which is what Mom called it, and I just wish I could go back in time."

That one sentence holds so much weight. "You know you're not alone, right? I'm here, your uncle is here, and we love you."

Looking at Morgan hurts a little. We used to joke that she was her mother's clone. They have the same eyes, hair color, and the dimple on her chin. More than that, she sees the world the way her mother did.

She scoots over on the bed, and I lie down next to her.

"I just wish things were different."

"I know, and I wish I could go back in time and change it for you." There's nothing I wouldn't do to ease her pain.

"It sucks."

It really does. "It'll get better, honey. Day by day, hour by hour, we'll all get through it."

"Do you promise?" she asks.

I take her hand in mine, and I swear I'm sixteen again.

"Why do you even like my brother?" Sabrina asks.

"Umm, because he's cute."

Seriously, everyone likes Ian. He's funny, hot, and really smart. He's the total package, but more than that, he looks at me like I'm special. I know I'm his little sister's annoying best friend, but when she's not around, I'm just London. Can't he see that?

"He's gross."

"Maybe to you." To my sixteen-year-old self, he's perfect.

Sabrina flops down on the pillow and turns toward me. "Promise me," she says, then stops.

"Promise you what?"

"Promise you'll always be my best friend. Even if he's a jerkface and is mean."

I roll over and wait for her to laugh, but she doesn't. "You're serious?"

She nods. "Do you promise?"

I don't know why she thinks anything would ever happen. Ian likes girls who are pretty, skinny, and don't have braces on. I'm definitely not his type. He's with Jamie Hardgrave who is the captain of the cheerleading squad, homecoming queen, and pretty much every teenage boy's fantasy. "I promise because I will never be with Ian."

Sabrina rolls back over. "I bet you one day he'll try to date you and then you'll be all, 'oh Ian . . .'" She clutches her chest. "I love you, Ian, even if you're an idiot."

I nearly choke on my laughter. "You're so stupid."

"I'm serious, London. Watch."

She says that like it's a bad thing, when it's everything I want. "Whatever."

"You're my best friend in the world," Sabrina says.

"And you're mine."

"At least if you guys get married, we'd be sisters."

I roll my eyes. "Don't get ahead of yourself! It's never going to happen, anyway. He's going to marry Jamie and have two kids and a dog."

She scoffs. "Yeah right. He's only dating her because Chad wanted her. I heard him say something on the phone about breaking up with her. Boys are so dumb."

I try to keep myself in check, but the idea is swirling around now. Ian and me . . . together.

"Yeah," I agree. "So dumb. Thank God we have Jason Priestley and Luke Perry to dream about."

Sabrina lets out a dramatic sigh. "Right. I want to find a man like one of them."

The memory fades, and I open my eyes. Morgan is breathing deeply and steadily next to me, sound asleep. I kiss the top of her head and snuggle closer to her. That's when I notice the mirror on the ceiling.

Fucking Ian.

Sighing, I carefully slip off Morgan's bed and exit the room. But there's no sense in being angry with him. He is who he is, and he never planned on being a father to these kids. Or any kids, as far as I know. He's going to need me, and he knows it.

Part of me likes that a little too much.

CHAPTER SEVEN
ian

I carry a sleeping Ruby up to the room she chose—refusing to look in the corner that previously housed the sex swing—and lay her down on the bed. However, she's still dressed. Do I leave her in her clothing? Try to get her into her pajamas? Wake her up to change?

I stand there for a moment, scratching my head and staring down at this poor little thing whose heart is so broken about the loss of her parents that she's lost her voice. And where did London say I had to drive her? Was it dance class? And Morgan . . . something about a science project? And Christopher—he plays basketball. That I know for sure because I've been to plenty of his games, but I'm going to have to be better at keeping track of all their activities. I'm all they've got now.

Feeling overwhelmed, I sit down on the edge of the bed.

I'm going to need London. There is no question; I can't get along without her. I can learn and I can try—and I will—but all this nurturing stuff comes so naturally to her.

I wonder why she never got married and had her own kids since she loves these three so much. Is it because of her career? That has to be it. She's always been so driven to succeed. How could she possibly have thought she would have been happy giving up her full ride to Northwestern just to stay here and fuck around with me?

I remember the night she told me about it. I was home from UNLV for the weekend, and Sabrina begged me to drag them along to a party I was going to. I said okay, though I was sure they were just going to bug me all night, and I'd spend the entire time ignoring them. But I couldn't get over how different London seemed that night—so confident and sexy. She had just been offered the full ride to Northwestern, and was also considering offers from like seven other fantastic schools. I remember looking at her and thinking how hot it was that this beautiful girl was so smart and driven. The kind of girl who was too good for me or any other jackass at that party.

And she liked me. I knew she did because Sabrina had hinted at it before, but I had never cared. That night, I looked at her differently. I kissed her out in someone's backyard behind a giant palm tree. I wanted to do more, but I told myself not to be a dick to her. She wasn't just some sorority girl at a party—she was my sister's best friend, and she trusted me.

Beside me, Ruby stirs in her sleep, rolling on to her side. She seems a little uncomfortable in her clothes, so I decide to try getting her into her pajamas. Her suitcase is open on the floor, and I switch on the lamp before pawing through it. Locating what I think is a nightgown, I bring it over to the bed. Then I take a deep breath and get started.

First, I peel off Ruby's little white socks. She doesn't even move. Congratulating myself, I move on to her shorts. It takes some effort to slide them down her legs, but I go slow and eventually manage to get them off. I'm totally sweating. Wiping my forehead with my forearm, I figure I probably need to get her into a sitting position to get her T-shirt off. I sit down on the bed, reach beneath her arms and bring her toward me. Immediately she flops forward with her head on my shoulder. Somehow, God knows how, I manage to get the shirt off one arm at a time and then over her head.

She wakes up. "Daddy?" she says, confused as she sits up and looks at me in the semi-dark.

"No, sweetie. It's Uncle Ian." Quickly I reach for the nightgown and put it over her head. She gets her arms in the sleeves and tips over backward as soon as it's on. I tug it down and cover her with the blankets before leaning over to kiss her forehead. Her panda bear—what was it? Ed? Fred?—has fallen to the floor, so I pick it up and tuck it in beside her. Then I switch off the lamp and turn toward the door.

And stop.

London is in the doorway, backlit by the light from the hall. She's leaning on the frame, arms crossed, and it's clear she's just watched the entire bedtime routine like a show.

"Bravo," she whispers as I get closer. "I'm impressed."

"I'm sweating," I admit as she moves aside so I can get by.

She laughs a little, following me into the hall. "The trick is to get her into her jammies before she's asleep."

"So I gathered. The other kids asleep?"

"Morgan is. Christopher might still be awake but he's in bed."

"I'll just check on them real quick."

"Okay. I'll wait downstairs."

"It's late, and it's been a long day. You don't have to stay."

She's already heading down the steps, but she looks up at me, and for a second I see the eighteen-year-old girl she used to be. The one I gave up. "I don't mind," she whispers. "And we should set up a schedule. Kids need routine."

I nod. "Right. Okay, I'll be down in a minute."

At the end of the hall is the room Christopher chose, and by the time I look in on him, he's sound asleep. I pull the door shut behind me and peek into Morgan's room, cringing at the mirror on the ceiling, but glad to see she's sleeping peacefully as well.

I switch off the hall light and head downstairs, where I find London sitting at the kitchen table with a pad of paper and a pen. She looks up at me. "All good?"

"All good." I take the seat diagonal from her, at the head of the table.

"So, tomorrow is Thursday. School day."

"Do they have to go?"

She gives me a look. "Yes, Ian. It's the law. They've been out for two weeks already. They need the routine and distraction. Now, over at my house I have the schedule that Sabrina gave me before she left for Hawaii." Her voice catches, her eyes closing. "Sorry. Need a second."

I reach over and touch her forearm, forgetting for a moment that I'm annoyed with her for being bossy. "It's okay. We're all going to need time."

After a couple deep breaths, she opens her eyes and goes on. "I'll get you a copy of that schedule, which has everything on it."

"Thanks." I take my hand back.

"But I thought maybe we could try to work out a plan for when you'll need me."

"Easy. Nights and weekends."

Another give-me-a-break look. "Ian. No. You cannot be gone every single night and every weekend."

"It's my job, London. Sabrina knew that."

"Maybe she thought you'd change your lifestyle if something happened to her."

I shrug. "Well, I can't. How did she think I was going to support the kids if I don't work? I run a club. That means nights and weekends."

London exhales like she's trying to be really patient with me. It's aggravating as fuck. "Work with me here, please. What nights would you be willing to take off? I would be willing to commit to being here Tuesdays and Thursdays and Saturdays for now. Can you handle the other nights?"

"No fucking way." I sit back and cross my arms. "That's four nights a week away from the club, including Fridays."

"So what nights are you willing to give up at the club?"

In the spirit of cooperation, which I'm trying to have, I give it some thought. "Mondays." The club was closed that night anyway.

She waits for me to go on. "And?"

"That's it. Mondays. Every other night is busy."

"Come on, Ian. Surely someone else can pour shots and gawk at fake tits at least one other night during the week."

"Fuck you, London." And fuck the spirit of cooperation. "Is that what you think I do?"

She shrugs.

"Running a club is hard work, and I have a hand in every facet of the operation—the finances, the licenses, the hiring and firing, stocking the bar, keeping the lights on, booking music, managing crowds. I have to deal with investors, the government, the health and fire department, the police, fucking temperamental DJs, and drunk-ass customers harassing my staff and each other. I don't just sit around on my ass and doodle numbers all day." I'm sick and tired of people thinking my job isn't work.

London slams the pen down on the table, her face flaming with anger. "Screw you. I work my ass off every single day, ten times harder than any man would have to in my position."

"Which is what again?" I know exactly what she does, I just want to piss her off. "Aren't you some kind of accountant?"

"I'm a revenue analyst." If looks could kill. "In a forty-billion-dollar industry."

"Oh. Well, good for you. But that sounds like a nice nine-to-five job that doesn't require you to be on site until four in the morning. Now, I can maybe swing Mondays and Wednesdays. But I need you the other nights. Your cat will just have to get along without you."

I'm ready for the explosion, but she doesn't blow up at me. Instead she sits back in her chair, closes her eyes, and takes a breath. "Ian. We have to stop this."

She's right, which only adds to the list of things about her irritating me right now. I shift in my chair. "Fine."

"You're going to have to hire a manager. Even if I have the kids those other nights."

"Don't tell me what to do." But in my gut, I know she's likely right about that as well. I won't be able to work the hours I have been and give the kids what they need. It has to be my idea, though, not her bossing me into it.

"Fine." She pushes back from the table and stands up. "I'm exhausted, and I have to work tomorrow. I'm going home. I'll drop the schedule in your mailbox in the morning."

I can't resist. "I'll be sure to memorize it. Will there be a quiz on Friday?"

Shaking her head, she walks toward the sliding door. "I'll be here by six tomorrow night. Good night, Ian."

"London, wait."

She pauses halfway there but doesn't turn to look at me.

"Look. I'm exhausted too, and sad, and worried about the kids, and overwhelmed at the thought of being a parent, and frankly just as surprised as you are that Sabrina chose me."

That makes her turn and face me. "You are? That's not what you said—"

"I know what I said." We keep looking at each other, the attraction between us simmering just beneath the antagonism, like it always has. "But she must have had her reasons, and I want to live up to them. It's just going to take me some time. Can I count on your help?"

"Of course you can. It's what she would have wanted me to do."

I get the message loud and clear. *I'm doing this for her, not for you.* And maybe I deserve it after the way I've treated her over the years, but dammit, she didn't leave me any choice. If I couldn't have her, I had to hate her. It was the only way I could get over her.

But as I sit here and watch her leave my house, I know that deep down, I never did.

The next morning, I'm awakened by the sound of high-pitched voices and clanking dishes. The master suite is on the first floor, just down the hall from the kitchen, and I left my bedroom door open last night just in case one of the kids woke up and called for me. This seemed very big of me at the time, but now I regret it.

I roll over and check the clock. Not even six-thirty. Fucking hell.

My room is still completely dark because of the blackout shades, but unless I get up and shut the door, the noise is going to keep me awake. I shove my head under the pillow and try to block it out, but a few seconds later I hear something shatter on the tile floor, followed by the sound of someone bursting into tears.

I jump out of bed and race down the hall to the kitchen, where Ruby, still in her nightgown, is standing over the remains of a glass, and Morgan is sitting at the counter eating a slice of cold pizza. She's also drinking a can of Coke.

"Ruby, sweetie, it's okay." I kneel down, careful to avoid the shards. "I don't care about the broken glass. We can clean it up."

She cries harder, tears streaming down her face. I pick her up and set her on the counter, then look around the kitchen. Do I own a broom? If so, where would it be?

"Uncle Ian, your hair is funny." Morgan is grinning at me.

I run a hand through it. "Thanks."

"What are you looking for?"

"A broom." I go over to the pantry and look inside. No luck.

"I'll find it." She hops off the stool and comes hurrying around the counter.

"Wait, Morgan, don't step on the—"

"Ouch!" Morgan picks up one foot and looks at the bottom of it. A piece of glass has sliced her arch, and she begins to cry as blood trickles from the wound.

Oh, Jesus. Okay, make a plan. Blood first, then clean up the glass. I know where the Band-Aids are, right? I open the drawer I thought they were in, but don't see them. Dammit!

"Okay, Morgan, just stay right there," I tell her, opening every drawer in the kitchen. "Don't move, I don't want you to step on any more glass." Fuck me, why didn't I keep Band-Aids somewhere more handy? Meanwhile, Ruby is still howling away on the counter.

In the middle of all this, the doorbell rings.

What the hell? At six o'clock in the morning? What sane person is up at this hour? Sidestepping the glass, I hurry to the door and look through the peephole.

Of course. London. I look down at my naked chest, pajama pants, and bare feet. I know my hair is a mess. In the kitchen, I've got two crying girls, one broken glass, one bloody foot, and a breakfast of pizza and Coke. I am not exactly winning the morning.

Oh, well. I open the door.

"Good morning, sunshine," I say as I look at her. She's completely ready for a day of work. The sun blinds me from behind her and the sound of the kids still screaming from the kitchen stops her from saying anything.

"What the hell?" London asks as she pushes her way through the front door and rushes into the kitchen.

Well, there goes any shred of hope that I don't look like a total fucking loser. I couldn't even last one night.

"Come on in." I close the door behind her.

"Ian!"

At least I'm consistent at disappointing her. I walk to the kitchen where she has Ruby in her arms and is looking at Morgan's foot.

"I swear, this isn't what it looks like," I try.

She shoots me a glaring look and I shrug. "Can you please get the first aid kit?" London's lips barely move as she asks through gritted teeth.

I don't say anything about her looking like a wooden dummy

—she might throw one of the shards at my head, and she was all-state in softball.

The kit is not in the obvious places like the kitchen or master bath. Where the fuck is it? I head into the guest bathroom and find it in the first drawer.

Score!

"Found it!" I yell like the hero I am and hustle down the stairs. "I found it!"

London rolls her eyes. "Good job. I got the glass out, you need to clean it and put a Band-Aid on."

I walk over to Morgan and restrain myself from flicking her in the nose. "I told you not to move."

Her arm moves across her nose and she sniffs. "You looked pissed that you couldn't find the broom. I was helping."

"I appreciate that, but next time listen." I wipe the tear with my thumb. "What were you doing down here so early anyway?"

"We were hungry. We have to eat."

"Before the sun is up?"

London huffs. "I know you're part vampire, but you have kids now, and they eat breakfast by seven. Maybe I should've brought the schedule over last night."

I put the bandage on Morgan's foot and help her down. "I would say so since we've had a fucking shitshow of a morning."

"Ian," she scolds as she lifts Ruby in her arms. "You're going to have to watch your mouth around them."

Yeah, that's going to be an issue.

I own a fucking nightclub. It's sex, drinking, and cursing.

"Or they need to learn not to repeat me."

She gives me a pointed stare. "Or you can be the adult here and act like the shining example Sabrina and David thought you would be to their three precious children."

Morgan clears her throat. "I'll take Ruby upstairs and get dressed. Sorry we broke the glass, Uncle Ian."

"Accidents happen," London answers.

I turn and glare at her. "Thanks, *Uncle Ian*." My sarcasm is clear. I turn back to Morgan and smile. "It's fine. I was more worried about you and Ruby. Go get your sister ready and wake your brother up in the most annoying way you can find."

Her grin grows and she takes her sister upstairs.

"Do you really think that was a good idea?" London asks when they're out of earshot.

"What?"

"Encouraging her to wake him up in some rude way."

"Do you remember the fucking crazy shit you and Sabrina would do to me on the weekends?"

My parents had this ridiculous rule that we eat breakfast together on the weekends. No one could touch a piece of food until the entire house was awake. Sabrina and I took joy in waking up at six in the morning just to find the most horrendous way to get the other person up. She was a master with shaving cream and I always ended up getting it in the face. It turned into all-out wars in our house. I feel it's only right that we pass on the tradition no matter what day of the week it is. That was part of parenting, right? Passing on traditions?

"Yes, I remember, but that doesn't mean you should encourage them to do the same," she scolds me.

London just loves a chance to prove she's right. I can't help but find ways to piss her off by using anything at my disposal to do the opposite.

"But where would the fun in that be?"

"You're such a child," London huffs. "I brought these over for the kids. I figured you didn't have a chance to go to the store last night." She reaches into her bag and takes out a box of breakfast bars.

"The food will be delivered at eleven, you know, when vampires tend to wake up," I joke and nudge her.

"Can you please get dressed?"

I look down at my chest and grin. "Am I making you uncomfortable?"

"No."

"Really?" I taunt.

I see her pupils dilate with lust, but she tries to hide it. "You know what, why don't you take your pants off, too? I mean, what almost-teenager doesn't want to see their uncle half naked?"

London is like a jack-in-the-box, you wind her up and then wait for her top to blow. It's fun and a little too easy. I know my bare chest is making her nervous by the way she keeps shifting her long legs and gripping her neck.

"Morgan has seen me in a bathing suit," I remind her.

"Different."

I move closer to her, keeping my eyes locked on hers. "Are you thinking about when I kissed you?"

Her lips part. "No."

I keep walking toward her, waiting for her to stop me. "No? You don't want me to hold you in my arms, press my lips to yours, and remind you how good we fit?" She doesn't move and now we're just a breath apart.

I could kiss her right now.

I could do everything I've wanted to.

But I won't make a fool of myself again.

"No, I don't."

She's lying, but I'll let her have it.

"The next time I kiss you, London Parish, it'll be because you beg me to," I promise her.

Her breathing is labored as her breasts brush against my bare chest.

She lets out a hearty laugh, and presses her hand to my chest, pushing me back. "That won't be happening anytime soon, but I appreciate the offer."

Disappointment floods me, but I don't let her see. Instead I give her a knowing grin. "Anytime, princess."

I turn around, close my eyes, and get myself back to the cocky prick she expects.

CHAPTER EIGHT
London

"Holy fuck!" I say as I slump against the wheel of my car. We were so close to doing something stupid again. Why am I such a dumbass lately? It's like this box has been opened and we don't know how to close it. It needs to be sealed shut and buried, with no hopes of being found again.

I sit up, looking at the house, and promise myself this stops here.

My job requires my full attention from this moment on. No more thoughts of kisses, abs that look more painted-on then real, or the feel of his fingers on my skin. Nope. It's all in the past. I'm back to being badass London Parish, kicker of all other analyst asses. Today I close a major deal because my career is riding on it.

I make a good living, but it's because I get the contracts signed, perform above their hopes, and get a referral from each one. I don't have time for Ian and whatever feelings I've buried getting resurrected. And of all the days, today is the one I need to be on my game.

Thankfully, my day is so insanely busy I don't have a moment to think about my personal life. Between checking everything I'd already prepared, checking it again, and then not throwing up in my meeting, my mind has been laser focused.

And I killed it.

I was better than ever before.

"Great job, London," my boss says as he sits in my office. "You really impressed him."

I had a meeting with the owner of the biggest casino chain in Las Vegas, and it went fantastic. He was funny, insightful, and needed me to go over some numbers that weren't adding up. It was a great opportunity, and the fact that he even knew of our firm is amazing in and of itself.

I smile. "Thanks, it felt good. I'm sending the contracts over to him tomorrow."

Casey gets to his feet and puts out his hand. "Way to seal the deal. Congrats again."

"I'm glad it worked out," I say, giving him a firm handshake.

"We didn't doubt it would, that's why you got this pitch." He smiles and then walks out.

I grab my phone and start typing to Sabrina, letting her know how amazing today was.

Me: OMG! I think I got the account I was going for! I'm so happy! Thank you for the tip about writing up the pitch on his yearly savings instead of quarterly. The bigger number definitely swayed him. You're the best.

And then I stare at the text.

I didn't think.

I didn't remember.

She'll never get the text.

My finger hovers over the send button, and then I backspace over every letter as the tears stream down my face.

I open the photo album on my phone and look at the last picture we took together. We were at Ian's pool when he was at work. He had no idea we were there until Sabrina set off the alarm and we ran back to my house, dripping wet, and laughing the entire time. We're standing on my deck, with the pool behind us, with our hands over our lips.

Not wanting Ian to know, I made her send me the photo and then delete it from her phone. She would've sent it to him because she loved making him crazy by ignoring his wishes. I also didn't want to have any reason to interact with Ian unless absolutely necessary.

But suddenly I have the urge to send him the pic, to let him know I had gotten away with something at his expense.

Me: I thought you might want to see what happened a few weeks ago when the cops had to go to your house. <photo attached>
Ian: You think I didn't know it was you two?

I smile, knowing he had no clue.

Me: Please, you didn't know!
Ian: <3 photos attached>

There's a photo of me and Sabrina in the pool, one of us running off the deck with our clothes in our arms, and the last one is of me staring right at his security camera with a huge grin.

I burst out laughing, wiping away the sad tears that were there just a moment ago.

Me: You knew!
Ian: I know everything.
Me: Let's not get too far ahead of ourselves.

Ian: I let you keep your secrets, but you two idiots cost me $400 in a false alarm fee from the city.

I laugh again, thinking how Sabrina would taunt him about how if he didn't have such a cool house, we wouldn't break in. Or how if he gave her a key and didn't change the codes once a week, then all of it would've been avoided.

Me: I should get back to work. I'll see you later.

Ian: Thanks for sending me that photo. I'm happy to see your faces that way instead of the criminals you both are as you sneak off my deck.

I turn the phone to selfie mode and make a kissy face.

Me: Instead of the customary one of me flipping you off, I thought this would be a nice change. <photo attached>

I have no idea why I did that, but it feels nice to talk to Ian and have it not end up in some argument. Maybe we can be friends.

Maybe we can find some sort of relationship where we're not clawing each other's eyes out or ripping each other's clothes off. That would be nice considering we're going to be around each other a lot.

Maybe.

～

"What time will you be home?" I ask as Ian stands in front of the mirror in his bedroom, looking unbelievably hot.

He's wearing a navy suit, brown shoes, and a light blue shirt with the top two buttons open. Seriously, I'm glad I'm usually watching CSI by the time he leaves for work or I'd probably be like a dog staring out the window each day just to catch a glimpse of him.

"Usually I'm home by four," he says as he fixes a piece of stray hair.

"Four?" I scream. "In the morning?"

He looks over as though I'm a total idiot. "What did you think?"

"I don't know," I admit. "Like maybe midnight?"

Ian tosses his head back and laughs. "Are you kidding?"

"I don't exactly go clubbing, Ian."

"The club doesn't get busy until midnight. I'll be here before you have to leave for work," he assures me.

That's not the problem. "That's great, but where the hell am I supposed to sleep?"

He looks perplexed for a moment and then shrugs. "You can sleep in my bed."

No.

No fucking way.

"Not happening."

"Well, all the guest rooms are now the kids' bedrooms. You're welcome to the couch, but five nights a week that's going to get a little old, don't you think?"

My life has gone to complete shit thanks to him. I have a beautiful home that I bought all on my own. It has three bedrooms, a huge four-poster king-size bed that is clean and untarnished by bodily fluids. I can't sleep in his bed.

I can't lay in the place that is all . . . him.

"There has to be another option. I really don't want chlamydia or whatever else is on that mattress."

Ian chuckles. "Just think, it'll be the closest you've been to having sex in a long time."

"You're such a pig. I could have sex if I wanted! There's no shortage of offers," I tell him.

"Your vibrator doesn't count."

I slap his arm. "Stop it. I'm serious. If I'm going to be helping you, I need somewhere to sleep."

He sighs and grips the back of his neck. "Look, I'm doing the best I can, but creating a bedroom for you is not on my very long list. This afternoon I ended up taking Ruby to basketball and Morgan to dance. Christopher's friend thankfully saw him after school and took him to practice."

I open my mouth and shake my head. "You fucked that all up, huh?"

"Yup."

There's no denying that he's trying, but . . . I'm not sleeping in his bed.

Ian walks over, lifts his hand, and drops it before it touches me. "No one has been in my bed since Sabrina's death, it's clean. My housekeeper came today, and she's coming three times a week now. You don't have to worry about that, okay? If you want to sleep on the couch, that's fine, but my bed is there if you change your mind."

My stomach clenches as I think about the last time we were in the same bed. It didn't end well.

We made promises.

We made love.

I learned heartache.

"I'll think about it," I tell him as I look away.

"You okay?" he asks.

I turn back, my mask back in place. "I'm fine. You should get going."

We walk down the hall to where Ruby is still working on her dinner, and he kisses the top of her head. "Be a good girl for Aunt London. I'll see you in the morning, preferably after six if you can manage that."

Ruby smiles at him. "Bye, Uncle Ian!"

My heart sputters at the fact that she just talked to him. Please let this mean this beautiful little girl is going to heal a little.

His eyes go wide and he smiles. "Bye, Ruby. I love you."

"Lub you!"

He gathers her in his arms, and I watch with my hand on my chest. She clings to him as I watch the emotions play across his face.

Ian walks to me with a huge grin. "She talked."

"I know."

"To me," he says, looking over at her. "Two weeks and the kid finally talked."

"Well," I say with a little smugness. "She never stopped talking to me."

Ian laughs a real, effortless laugh and it makes me smile. It's the man I fell for all those years ago. When he wasn't trying to be a dick all the time.

"You're just special, Lon."

"Yeah, don't forget it." I tap his chest.

His eyes meet mine and the carefree joking we had a moment ago vanishes. There's heat in his gaze and my pulse roars in my ears. "I never forgot, I just couldn't tell you the truth."

Every breath I take makes my chest tight. "What's the truth?"

"That he likes you!" Morgan yells from the living room and we both take a step back.

"You have horrible timing!" Ian points to the twelve-year-old that seems hell-bent on driving her uncle to drink.

"I always knew I liked that kid."

He raises one brow and lifts his lip in a smirk. "Yeah, what's not to love?" he says loud enough so she'll hear.

"I'm your favorite, just admit it."

Ian and I laugh at Morgan and then he looks at his watch. "I have to go."

"We'll be fine."

"Call me if you need me."

I nod. "I'll see you in the morning."

He leans in close, touches my cheek, and his voice is a barely a whisper. "Sleep on the left side of the bed, and don't wait up."

I slap his hand away. "Very funny. I'll be on the couch when you get home, thank you very much."

Giving me one more of his cocky grins, he picks up a leather messenger bag from the floor near the front door, slings it over his shoulder, and heads out.

As soon as the door shuts behind him, I exhale and fan my face. Damn him for looking so good in that suit. And for telling me to sleep in his bed. And for putting all kinds of terrible ideas in my head.

I cannot let him get to me.

I head back to the kitchen and start loading the dishwasher, asking Ruby about her day at school and her upcoming dance recital. While I'm thinking about it, I grab my phone from my purse and text Ian the dates.

Me: Friday, June 16th and Saturday, June 17th are Ruby's dance recitals. You'll have to get that weekend off or go in late.

Since he's still driving to work, he won't reply for a while, so I set my phone aside. "How's the homework coming, Morgan?" I ask.

"Fine," she says from the couch. "I finished math and science, now I just have to read."

"Aunt London, can I be done?" Ruby gives me a plaintive look from her chair at the counter.

I take a look at her plate and see that she's eaten most of her chicken nuggets and macaroni and cheese. "Ruby, what else did you have for dinner? Did Uncle Ian make you any vegetables?"

"No. He said we could pick what we wanted."

Of course he did. He probably told them to cook it themselves, too. Sighing, I pick up her plate and carry it to the sink.

"Well, you should have something healthy. Can I slice an apple for you?"

"Okay."

I take an apple from the bowl of fruit on the counter, which I'm happy to see because it means he at least purchased some healthy options from the store. Now I just have to get him to understand that the kids need to actually *eat* them. After cutting it up, I put half the slices on a plate for Ruby and bring the other half to Morgan in the living room. While they nibble on them, I prepare a plate for Christopher, since I know he'll be hungry when he gets home from basketball—pasta and meatballs with tomato sauce, and broccoli with lemon. The meatballs were frozen and the sauce is from a jar, but it's better than what the girls ate. There are enough leftovers for dinner tomorrow night, or even for Ian to eat when he gets home from work if he's hungry. I put it all into plastic containers, label them with sticky notes, and put them in the fridge. When that's all done and the kitchen is clean, I ask the girls if they have any laundry they need done.

"Yes," calls Morgan. "It's in my room on the floor."

Of course it is.

"Ruby, what about you?" She's still wearing her leotard and tights from dance class, but I know she'll need them again for Saturday. "Do you need me to wash your ballet clothes? Or do you have extra?"

"I have extra. Can I color?" she asks, sliding off her chair.

"Sure, honey." We locate some paper and the art supplies Sabrina's mom had the foresight to pack up and bring here from their house, and I leave her sitting at the kitchen table.

Then I grab my phone and find a message from Ian.

Ian: Don't tell me what to do, woman.

Idiot. But I'm grinning.

Me: I wouldn't have to if you were a grown up all the time.
Ian: Growing up is overrated.
Me: Clearly.
Ian: Heading to the back room where I have no service. But I have one question, do you sleep naked?

Oh my God. He's so ridiculous.

Me: You'll never know.

Ian has a first-floor laundry room off the hallway between his bedroom and the kitchen, and I grab an empty basket from it and head upstairs, still smiling from our text exchange. In Morgan's room, it's just as she says—clothes are everywhere, and I can hardly tell what's dirty and what's clean. I guess as well as I can, sticking some things in the basket and folding the rest, placing things in drawers. In Ruby's room, I find her nightgown and school clothes on the floor, and add them to the basket.

Christopher's room already smells like a teenage boy, and I'm a little leery about invading his privacy, so I skip it, deciding I'll simply stick an empty basket in his room and let him fill it.

Back in the laundry room, I fill the washer and turn it on before joining Ruby at the table.

"What are you making?" I ask as she sprinkles glitter glue on her picture.

"A princess. It's for Uncle Ian," she tells me. "He can take it to work."

I smile, imagining him hanging up the glittery pink artwork in his office. "That's so nice of you. He's going to love it."

My phone has another missed text.

. . .

Ian: I'm pretty sure I already know, but can't wait to see if I'm right.

My stomach flutters thinking about the two of us in any bed again. I shut it down, though. That's a thought I don't need to entertain.

Ian is bad for my heart.

CHAPTER NINE

London

Christopher comes in around seven and gobbles up dinner like he hasn't eaten in days. After a second helping, he heads upstairs to shower without saying much. I'm concerned about him, but I don't want to push. He doesn't come back downstairs, and when I take Ruby up to bed at eight and then Morgan at nine-thirty, he's still in his room with the door shut. After debating whether or not I should just leave him be for now, I decide to knock.

"Christopher?"

"Yeah?" His voice is muffled through the closed door.

"Everything okay?"

"Yeah."

"Well... do you need anything?"

"No."

I bite my lip. "Okay, honey. I put an empty laundry basket in your closet earlier. You can use that for your dirty clothes."

"Thanks."

I give it a few more seconds but can't think of anything else to draw him out, and maybe he needs the alone time, anyway. "Goodnight. I'm here if you need anything."

"Night."

Folding my arms over my chest, I head back downstairs to switch the girls' laundry into the dryer, but there's a load of Ian's darks in there. Tossing it into a basket, I transfer the girls' things into the dryer and turn it on. Then, since I am the type of person who cannot stand to leave clean clothes heaped in a basket, I figure I might as well fold Ian's things.

I bring the basket out to the living room, sit on the couch, and turn on CSI. As I work, it occurs to me this evening offers a little glimpse of what my life might have been like had things not gone so wrong with Ian and me. We might be married now. We might live in a big house like this with a pool. We might have three amazing kids like the ones sleeping upstairs. I might be here folding laundry on a Thursday night while he's at work. I cringe a little at the traditional gender roles implied in this scenario—I like being a woman with a career—but the feeling is actually kind of nice. Cozy. Reassuring. And who's to say I wouldn't be getting up in the morning and hurrying into the office once I got the kids on the bus? Women don't have to choose these days, do they?

I've folded a few shirts and matched a couple pairs of socks when I realize the load also contains a few pairs of underwear—short boxer briefs in navy and black. My stomach flutters a little as my mind wanders deeper into the fantasy. Maybe when he gets home, I'm already asleep in bed, but he slips in behind me and curls his warm body around mine. Maybe I feel him start to get hard as his hands move over my breasts. Maybe I reach behind me and wrap my hand around his cock and he says to me, his voice deep and gravelly in the dark, "Want something?" Then he—

"Aunt London?"

I open my eyes, realizing Ruby has just caught me swooning over a pair of men's underpants. Shoving them behind my back, I clear my throat. "What is it, sweetie?"

"I'm thirsty. Can I have some water?"

"Of course." I jump up, and she follows me to the kitchen. My nipples are hard and tingling, and my underwear feels damp. I focus on filling a glass with water and shove the thought of Ian naked and hard and reaching for me out of my mind.

It's not easy.

I give the glass to Ruby. "Here you go."

After she's taken a couple sips, she hands it back. "Thank you."

"You're welcome, sweetie. Come on, I'll tuck you back in." I hold her hand and take her back up to bed, and when I pass Christopher's room on my way back down the hall, I notice the light is still on and I hear muffled sobs. My heart squeezes, and tears come to my eyes. These poor kids. I knock twice, softly.

The crying stops, but he doesn't say anything.

"Chris, honey? Can I come in?"

"No!"

I try the handle anyway. Locked. "Please, Christopher. Let me in."

"I'm fine. Go away."

"I'm sorry, but I can't. So if you won't let me in, I'll just sit right here and wait for you to come out. I'll stay all night if I have to." I plop down on the hall carpet, legs crisscrossed.

A moment later, he opens the door. His eyes are bloodshot, his nose red. "What do you want?"

"I want to talk to you." I scramble to my feet. "Can I come in?"

He sighs. "Fine."

I follow him into his room and perch on the edge of the dresser while he sits on the bed. "How are you feeling?"

He laughs, but it's bitter. "Great."

"You know, it's okay to cry when you're this sad."

"No, it's not."

"Of course it is, honey. Everyone cries when they're sad."

"Men don't." He sits up a little taller, his chest puffing out.

"Says who?"

"Uncle Ian. He told me men are fixers. Men are strong. Crying shows weakness."

Fury boils inside me. "That is ridiculous," I snap, standing up.

"A real man is not afraid to show his feelings, no matter what they are."

"That's not what he says. He told me men have to be strong for the women. I need to be strong for my sisters." He swipes at his nose with the back of his hand.

"You have every right to cry, honey. Your Uncle Ian is wrong." But I can tell Christopher doesn't believe me.

"Well, I don't want to cry," he says angrily. "I'm sick of it. I'm sick of being sad and people asking how I'm doing and telling me how sorry they are. It doesn't fucking matter. I just want to be left the fuck alone." He turns his back to me.

I could tell him to watch his language, but I don't. Anger will be part of the grieving process too, and it's not like his sisters are in the room. "Okay, Christopher. I'll leave you be. But if you change your mind, I'm here."

Leaving his room, I shut the door behind me and go back downstairs with a heavy heart. We're going to have to keep an eye on Christopher—he's a sensitive kid, and if he feels like he has to bottle up all his sad feelings, eventually they're going to be channeled into something else.

In the living room, I finish folding Ian's and then the girls' laundry, and place everything back in the baskets. The girls' basket I leave at the bottom of the stairs, but Ian's I take to his bedroom.

I planned to simply leave it on the floor in his walk-in closet and go back to the living room couch, but once I'm in there, I can't resist looking around a little. It's surprisingly neat—he hangs his work shirts by color, his shoes are lined up in tidy rows on two shelves, and his knits are nicely folded and stacked three deep. Gingerly, I pull open one drawer and find two piles of crisp white undershirts. The drawer beneath it holds colored T-shirts. A third reveals neat stacks of underwear. Belts and ties are hanging on cedar racks, all the hangers match, and nothing is out of place— no stray pair of jeans tossed over a hook, no workout wear flung on the floor, no sad, dirty sock crumpled and forgotten in the corner. It even smells good, like leather and wood and a faint whiff of cologne. I inhale deeply, and get a tingly feeling between my legs.

Yes, it turns me on that Ian's closet is so organized and clean. It also annoys me—who'd have thought that such an uncivilized caveman, one who believes men can't cry and thinks naked pool parties at three AM are perfectly acceptable, would turn out to have a neat streak? I decide that since I'm in there and can clearly see where everything goes, I might as well put away the laundry I've folded. As I do so, I try my best to ignore the nagging voice telling me I shouldn't like this so much. There's nothing wrong with doing a little favor for Ian, is there? After all, we're trying to get along better. It's not like I'm snooping or something. I'm being nice.

When I'm finished, I leave the empty basket in his closet. A bedside lamp is on low in his bedroom, and I can't resist wandering over to the bed.

I remember he told me to stay on the left side and I eyeball it warily, wondering how many women have spent the night there. Is Ian the sleepover type? Or is he more like the guy who has rules about staying over and calls a car for his conquests as soon as he's done with them?

Then I stare at the right side for a moment, imagining his sleeping form beneath the covers. Does he sleep on his stomach or back? Does he stay still during the night or move around? Does he sleep in pajamas or naked? My stomach whooshes, and I place a hand over it. It's been almost twenty years, but nothing, not even hating him, has erased the memory of his body on mine.

Enough. Get out of his bedroom. You don't belong here.

But after I've turned off all the downstairs lights and stretched out on the couch, I can't stop hearing his voice. *The next time I kiss you, London Parish, it'll be because you beg me to.*

I'm a little worried he might be right.

CHAPTER TEN

ian

"Don't you want me to come over to your place?" a half-drunk brunette, named Collette, who drives a Corvette, asks, while running her finger down my chest.

Any other night, the answer would've been, Why wait to get back to my place? I have an office and a lock. But tonight...

Nope.

I'm not even a little interested in this woman with legs for days.

Instead, my mind has been traveling back to a different brunette. Instead of blond highlights, the one I'm thinking of has chocolate brown hair with subtle red hues in it. Her green eyes are pure jade instead of the deep brown the woman in front of me has. And while Colette wants to be in my bed, I'm silently praying London is in my bed... naked.

"Not this time." I pull her hand away, and she pouts.

"Maybe tomorrow?"

"Maybe not," I say and take a sip of my drink.

Being back has been weird and working off the excess energy is exactly what I should do, but not like this. I'll run or go for a swim when I get back. Thankfully, my absence didn't cause the club any major issues, which is a good thing. It means Drea is actually doing her job—finally. Or, at least she didn't burn the place down. However, I spent a good part of the night fixing orders that were going out tomorrow. Drea is not so good when it comes to the paperwork part.

I came out to the floor about two hours ago, enjoying the atmosphere, talking with customers, and needing to get away from my phone since I checked it about a hundred times. I've become a pussy, waiting for a text message from a girl.

A girl that's not even my girl.

"If you change your mind . . ." She grins.

"I won't, but have a good night and get home safe."

Toby lets out a laugh that he attempts to cover over with cough, but I catch it. Collette walks out of the club, feelings probably hurt, but we're officially closed now. Tonight, we were packed, everything went great, and I felt like myself again, minus the not getting laid part.

"Don't say a word," I warn him, lifting my glass to get a little more. I've earned it.

I've known Toby a long time. He and I started out the same way, promoting the hottest clubs on the strip, partying at them so we could bring in more girls who would spend all their money. He's good people and I never have to worry about cash missing from the register.

He refills my scotch. "That's a first."

"I'm experiencing a lot of those lately."

First time driving a fucking minivan, dealing with a five-year-old who doesn't want to talk to me, remembering to feed other people, kissing London and thinking about doing it again . . . the list has been endless since Sabrina's death.

"Never thought I'd see the day," he laughs.

"Yeah, me either."

Giant. Fucking. Pussy.

That's the next tattoo I'm getting, right across my forehead.

"How is it having the kids in the house?"

"It's a mix of being tortured and being happy at the same time. This will be the real test, though."

"How's that?" he asks.

"Because now we go back to living life. I'm working, they're in school. We were sort of living in a world of false security before, you know?"

Toby's parents died when he was sixteen. Instead of going to a family member, he went into the system. No one wanted an emotionally fucked-up teenager, so he was pretty much between foster homes and on the street.

He told me a few stories back when we drank way too much in our early days.

"Look," he says as he stops wiping the counter. "You're doing a good thing. Whatever anyone says, you've got my respect. Those kids need you, and no matter what you're giving up, it's worth it."

Some days it feels like I've given up nothing. I may be an idiot most days, but I love those kids. There was never really a question of keeping them. Hell, even if Sabrina chose someone else, I would've been a part of their lives.

It's just that the timing that sucks. This club is brand new. It needs time and attention, just like the kids do.

Who the fuck thought I could handle this?

London didn't and maybe she was right. The fact is, even if she is right and I'm the wrong man for the job, I won't fail those kids. I love them too much, and they're all that's left of my sister now. I have to do right by her and prove that she was doing the right thing in choosing me over her best friend.

Then there's London. She's a whole other set of issues. Our relationship is changing, or at least the way I think about her is, which is scaring the shit out of me.

It's weird, because for so long I've focused on hating her, and now I can't seem to stop imagining being around her. She's a pain in my ass, but she's also saving it at the same time. If it weren't for her help, I'd be totally fucked.

I have to make sure those kids feel secure in their new life. London and I can at least agree that they come first.

"I appreciate it. Listen, I'm going to need some extra help around here. I'd like you to start training a new bartender so you can help out with more management stuff. My niece has some things coming up, and apparently it's an entire weekend where I'll need to take off. There will probably be a lot more of these too. I'd like to have you and Drea run the show when I need to be at home."

There's no one else I would trust to do this. He knows how this scene works and how to grow. Drea can manage the customer side and Toby can cover the business aspects when I'm gone.

"Are you sure? I mean, I'm cool with helping out, but . . ."

"Yeah, man, I'm sure."

"All right. There's a few bartenders from another club looking to make a change. I'll see if any are available on the nights you need me to do other stuff."

I look down at my watch and groan. "I need to get going, it's already three and I have to get the kids to school by eight."

He laughs. "Better you than me."

"It would be better if it was their parents," I say before draining my glass.

"Yeah, see you tomorrow, Ian."

I head out the back door, getting into my Porsche, and leaning my head back. I'm fucking beat. I'm used to long, late hours but I usually can sleep in. Now, I'm up at o'dark thirty and still have to stay up. Once I drop them off at school, I have no plans of getting out of bed.

A smile forms when I think about what might be waiting for me in that bed.

London Parish.

I want nothing more than to get home and find her lying there, hair spilled across my pillow. I'll crawl in behind her, wrap my arms around her, and then I'll fuck her senseless. If I can just get this crazy lust I feel for her out of my system, then maybe we can go back to normal.

Not wanting to wait another second, I start driving home.

It takes about fifteen minutes and when I turn on the street, the house is pitch black. Being as quiet as I can, I go inside.

First, I head upstairs, open each of the kids' rooms, and check on them. I don't know why, but being away from them was an oddly uncomfortable experience. I wondered if they were okay all night long. Did Morgan finish her homework? How was Chris's attitude? Did London make sure Ruby had her ratty panda to go to sleep with?

Then I thought about her.

Once I've checked on them all, I go to my room. I'm not sure if she took me up on the offer to sleep in my bed, so I use the light on my phone, but the bed is empty.

I should've known. She's way too fucking stubborn to give in. London would rather sleep on a bed of nails then be anywhere near me.

She has no idea that even after all this time, I still want her.

I walk out to the living room and sure enough, she's on the couch.

"Why can't you ever give in?" I ask quietly as I brush her hair back. "You make everything a fight."

Nothing has ever been easy with us. I hardened myself to everything pertaining to her once I fell on my sword to ensure she had the life she deserved. London would've lost everything if I hadn't walked away. Hurting her that day was the worst thing I've ever done, but it was the only option.

Still. It was like someone cut me open when I saw her tears at that party. She would never forgive me, and I'd never forgive myself.

I look down at her, hating that instead of sleeping where she'd be physically comfortable, she's here to be away from me.

Maybe I'll never be able to get her to see me differently. Should I even try?

"Fuck it," I mutter and lift her into my arms. She doesn't deserve to sleep on the couch.

"Ian?"

"Shhh," I tell her, holding her to my chest. "I've got you."

Her arms go around my neck and I breathe in her vanilla and almond perfume. I make my way to my room, being careful not to wake her again. When I place her down, her eyes shoot open.

"What? Ian?" She scrambles quickly across the bed. Away from me.

"Relax, it's fine. I'm going to sleep on the couch for a few hours, you stay here."

The moonlight hits her face and I have to stop myself from rushing over to her and kissing her until neither of us can breathe.

Has she always been this beautiful?

Yes, she has. I've just been too angry to see it. Her hair hangs down around her shoulders, brushing the tops of her breasts. It would be too easy to push her down, crawl on top of her, and make her beg for me.

London represents everything I've ever wanted but didn't deserve.

She's a pain in the ass, but she's also brilliant, funny, kind, and loving. I loved her once and let her go because she needed to fly.

Even in my selfish sex-crazed twenties, I knew that.

"No, no, this is your bed and . . ."

"Go to sleep, Lon. You should be comfortable."

"I can sleep on the couch."

"And so can I."

Stubborn. As. Fuck.

"What time is it?" she asks, looking around.

"It's about three-thirty. Get some rest, I'll see you in the morning." Leaning over her, I kiss her forehead and get up.

"Have it your way."

If I had it my way, I'd be next to her.

"This isn't my way," I tell her.

"Well," she sighs as she lies back on the pillow. "Thank you, I appreciate it."

Anything for you.

I push that thought out of my head. I can't seem to pull myself back anymore. All the feelings that were dead and gone have been resurrected. I want her. I've always wanted her, that was never the issue. It was that I've never been good enough for her. London is the sun, the stars, the light at the end of the tunnel that I'm so desperate to reach, but know I'll never touch. I have to remember that she dislikes me for good reason. If only she didn't look so beautiful in my bed...

"Goodnight."

I look over, shake my head, and shove the thoughts from my head. "Goodnight, London."

I hear the sheets move as she gets comfortable, and I need to get out of these fucking clothes and out of my head.

That's the one thing about nightlife in Vegas, you reek of it. It clings to you, reminding you of the booze, smoke, desperation, and perfume you enjoyed hours ago. I used to love that smell, but now, I want it gone.

I enter my closet, so I can put the light on and get what I need to shower. A laundry basket is sitting on the floor there. What the hell? I take my shirt and pants off, toss them in there and go to grab clothes.

Okay, this is fucking weird. My very neat and organized drawer has a pair of underwear in with my shirts. My housekeeper would never do that, and I was in here before work and this was not how things were.

I look around to make sure the sex toys are still in the kick drawer and untouched. Lord only knows what kind of questions I'd be facing in the morning if it was the kids.

Thankfully, nothing in that drawer was touched.

But still, I feel like some Goldilocks-and-the-Three-Bears-type shit is going on here.

I exit the closet and when London moves a little, I can't help wanting to know what the hell happened while I was at work.

"Did the kids come in here?" I ask London.

"Not that I know of," she mumbles, turning on her side. "Why?"

What kind of a babysitter is she if she doesn't even know if the kids came in here? We'll discuss that after we get to the bottom of my closet issue.

"Someone's been touching my clothes."

"What?"

"My shit is moved."

"You're insane."

"No," I correct her. "I'm right. Someone was snooping in my closet today because things aren't where they should be."

"Need sleep, Ian. I can't deal with your crazy right now. Bed."

"Okay, you want me to come to bed? Move over."

She leans up on her elbow, probably to chastise me, but then she covers her eyes with her hand. "Ian! You're naked!"

I look down. "I have boxers on."

"Well, get dressed."

"I will after I shower. Unless you'd like to get undressed and join me?"

London covers her face with the pillow and then groans. "Such an asshole."

I chuckle and decide this is too great of an opportunity to pass up. I climb up onto the bed, hovering over her, and start to tickle her sides.

"What did you call me?"

"Oh, my God! Stop!" She giggles, writhing underneath me. "Ian!" She slaps my arm.

The pillow goes flying, and I grin as I continue my assault "What did you say?"

"Asshole!" She bursts out in a fit of giggles and I stop.

"You're so beautiful when you laugh," I say, and she goes still.

I don't know why I said it, but I can't take it back, and I meant it. She *is* beautiful when she laughs. She's beautiful all the time, but I've done everything possible to stop seeing her that way.

"Ian." Her eyes stay on mine. "Don't say things you don't mean."

"I'm not. You're beautiful and you know it."

We both stare at each other. The laughter is gone and my cock is rock hard.

This isn't to shut her up.

This isn't a game.

I want her, and there's no way she doesn't feel that right now.

"This . . ." she starts to say, and then her hands move up my chest. "This isn't . . ."

"This isn't what?"

Her fingers inch up my neck, cupping the back of my head. "A good idea."

"Probably not." I run my hands up her side, waiting for her to tell me to stop. I touch every curve, feel her skin again.

She was always the smart one between the two of us. I was always the idiot. I hurt her and broke her heart, but I fucking destroyed myself at the same time. She never knew that. To her, I was the asshole who fucked her and never looked back. I made promises that were broken because I got what I wanted.

None of that was true.

I wanted her.

I wanted all of her.

I ended up losing any chance of that.

Fuck, I'm a fool.

"Tell me to stop," I command her as my hand gets closer to her chest. "Tell me now or beg for more."

"Stop." But her voice is breathless and her hands are in my hair.

"Stop what?" My left hand is inching up her ribcage, my thumb sweeping the underside of her breast.

"Confusing me."

I'm feeling brave enough—and turned on enough—to brush

my thumb over her nipple. It's hard enough to poke through her bra and her top, and when I touch it, she arches her back, inhaling sharply. "What are you confused about?"

Her fingers curl in my hair. "You. This. Us. There shouldn't be an us."

"Nope." I keep rubbing the stiff little peak with my thumb, and when she doesn't protest, I lift up her shirt. "There shouldn't."

"Oh, God," she whimpers as I lower my mouth to the fullest part of her breast. "That feels so good, but..."

Words seem to fail her as I pull down the lacy cup of her bra and stroke her nipple with my tongue. Once. Twice. Then in a lazy little circle.

"But what?" I reach behind her back, easy to do since it's bowed toward me, and unhook her bra with one hand.

"But we've been down this road before."

"It was a good trip, if I recall correctly." I slide my palms from her taut stomach up over both breasts. The light from my closet spills into the room, but she's still in shadow. Her skin is luminous in the dark. My cock is steel in my boxers. If she says no at this point, I will need a long, hot shower during which I will jerk off repeatedly to the memory of her beneath me in this bed, my hands on her perfect round tits.

"It was good," she murmurs, her eyes closing while I tease her nipples with my fingers. "But it ended so badly."

"It could be good again." I move to lie above her, settling my hips between her thighs. "Just for fun. Don't you think?"

"Oh, fuck." She can feel my erection through the soft, thin fabric of the yoga pants she's wearing. Judging from the way her hands go straight to my ass and pull me closer, I think she likes it. "You're so hard."

"Yes," I say, rolling my hips in a slow, sinuous motion, rubbing my cock against her sweet spot. I put my mouth right next to her ear and speak softly. "You shouldn't make me so hard, London. But you do. It's driving me fucking crazy how much I want you."

"But Ian." She slides her hands inside the waistband of my underwear. "We hate each other. Don't we?"

"That's right. We do." I lower my head to her throat and kiss my way down her chest. When I close my lips over one tight pink tip, she moans, bringing her hands back to my head. I suck at her greedily, continuing to rock my hips above her. Pretty soon my hands are dragging her pants and underwear off in one long swoop, and she doesn't stop me. In fact, she sits up and whips her shirt over her head and flings her bra to the floor.

"Take your boxers off," she demands breathlessly.

"Even in bed, you're bossy." But I do as she says, then kneel between her legs. My dick has hijacked my pride at this point. I will have this woman one way or another tonight, and I don't give a fuck about the circumstances.

"I like bossing you around." She reaches out and wraps her fingers around my cock, squeezing as she works her fist up and down my shaft.

"Yeah?" I'm momentarily paralyzed by how good it feels to have her hands on me, and for a second I'm afraid I might blow my load like a teenager.

"Yeah. You make it so easy." She dips her head down and swirls her tongue over my crown, and my dick twitches threateningly.

"Christ. Enough." I tip her backward and shimmy down her body until my head is between her thighs. "It's my turn to get bossy now."

"Oh, really?"

"Really." I give her a long, slow stroke with my tongue right up her center, lingering at the top, gratified by her tortured sigh. "Now here's what's going to happen. I'm going to make you come so hard with my tongue you won't even know what day it is. You're going to beg for more. You're going to beg for my cock. You're going to beg me to fuck you."

Just so she knows I mean what I say, I lick her firm, swollen clit again and then suck it gently into my mouth, flicking it with the tip of my tongue. Her hands claw the sheets. Her legs tremble. Her hips undulate beneath my jaw, and her moan grows so loud I know she's forgotten we're not alone in the house. "Good girl. But you're not allowed to scream, London, even though you're going to want to. I don't want to be interrupted tonight."

She whines faintly as I slip two fingers inside her, and my cock surges with envy at the tight, wet heat surrounding them. I can't help moving my hips, fucking the mattress like I want to be fucking her. I slide my fingers deeper, searching for the secret place that will put her over the edge, working her clit with my mouth. I know exactly when I find it.

"Oh, God, I hate you," she breathes, her body clenching around my fingers, her hands moving through my hair. I go at her even harder, and her hands curl into fists, pulling my hair so hard my scalp stings. "I hate you so much."

I'm fucking loving this.

"Oh, God, oh, God, oh my fucking God . . ." She drops her head to the side and whimpers softly, desperately trying to stay quiet as her body convulses and her clit beats repeatedly against my tongue. I keep going until I'm positive her orgasm is finished, then I back off and wipe my mouth with my forearm.

London props herself up on her elbows and looks at me like she can't decide whether to kick me or kiss me. It's hot as fuck.

"Say it," I demand, reaching over to the nightstand drawer for a condom. "Say you want more."

Her eyes are big and hungry as she watches me roll it onto my cock. Not gonna lie, it's pretty impressive. I can see she wants it, but she's torn between another orgasm and putting me in my place.

I'm betting the orgasm wins.

"Say it, London." I take my dick in my hand and rub the tip over her clit.

"I want more," she hisses.

I give her just the crown. "More what?"

"You know what."

I pull out. "You have to say it."

She glares at me, then growls the words I want to hear through clenched teeth. "I want your cock."

I slide inside her again, giving her a few solid inches past the crown, but not everything. "How much?"

"All of it. I want all of your cock." She doesn't even hesitate.

I like that.

Easing in all the way, slowly, because I'm not a complete jerkoff, I don't stop until I'm buried balls deep and she's dropped her head back on the pillow, breathing hard. I'm dying to move, and holding back is difficult, but I can't let her off the hook until I win this round. I know I said this wasn't a game, but she made it into one.

Victory is in sight as she wraps her arms and legs around me. "Now what do you want?" I whisper in her ear.

She digs her fingernails into my back, and the tension pulls tighter in me.

"Tell me, London."

She rakes them down either side of my spine and down over my ass.

"Tell me." Already my body is beginning to move of its own accord.

She tilts her hips and pulls me in deeper. "I want you to fuck me, you son of a bitch."

I would have laughed at the name-calling if I wasn't so out of my mind with need. It was just like her to try for the last word, even as she was doing exactly what I said she would.

The thought makes me almost delirious as I move inside her —I brought the high and mighty London Parish to her knees. I made her want me. I made her beg. She hates me, and here she is in my bed, naked and sweaty and panting my name, whispering the sweetest words I've ever heard out of her mouth.

"Oh, God, Ian, what are you doing to me?"

"Making you come again." I've changed the angle slightly so I can give her more of what she needs. Listening to her body is easy.

She moves freely and unabashedly, taking what she wants and unafraid to show how much she's enjoying it. It's such a contrast from the way she is in everyday life—and so fucking hot to me.

I don't want a lifeless blow-up doll in my bed, no matter how gorgeous she is. Give me London every time—feisty, greedy, passionate, playful. I remember that even as a shy seventeen-year-old girl, she'd been surprisingly fearless in bed, so much so that I told her I didn't believe she was a virgin. She swore she was, but said I made it easy for her to get carried away. The memory nearly makes me lose control.

"Yes, yes, yes," she breathes, her heels digging into the backs of my thighs as I fuck her harder and faster. "Right there, just like that."

Good thing, because the next few seconds has me going stiff as a board over her, groaning way too loudly as my cock throbs again and again. Thank fuck she comes right then too, her hands tight on my ass as her body spasms around me.

We probably woke up the kids.

Possibly even the neighbors' kids.

Possibly even the kids two time zones and seven states across the country.

I don't care. Worth it.

CHAPTER ELEVEN
London

Oh, dear.
      Oh, calamity.
Oh, my God.

I'm lying beneath Ian, crushed by his warm bare chest, his skin covered with a light sheen of sweat, just like mine is.

I want to tell him to get off me. I want to tell him I can't breathe. I want to tell him what we just did is a mistake and can't ever happen again—and I need to say it before he does.

"Ian. Move." I shove at his giant slab of a muscular torso. "I need air."

"Oh. Sorry." He lifts himself off me, pulling out and rolling onto his back.

I stay on my back too, still trying to catch my breath. I'm not quite sure how that just happened. Hadn't I gone to sleep on the couch in order to avoid this very problem?

Ugh, now I was one of them—those stupid, flighty girls who can't resist Ian's charms or his body or his big stupid dick.

His big, stupid, magical dick.

I squeeze my eyes shut and force myself not to think about it. Not its size or its talent or the way it felt pulsing deep inside me. Because its owner is not good for me. Those fantasies I had earlier in the night were just that—fantasies. Clearly I let them work me up a little too much, so much that I was unable to resist Ian's advances. He's probably laughing at me inside his head, congratulating himself on yet another conquest.

I sit up. "This was a mistake."

He looks at me. "It was?"

"Wasn't it?" I risk a glance at his face, but can't read his expression in the dark.

"I don't know. You said it."

"Because I think it was. And we can't do it again."

"Why not?"

"Ian. We can't stand each other most of the time. And we're supposed to be working on getting along for the kids' sake. Throwing sex into the mix will only complicate things further."

"You didn't enjoy it?"

"That's not the point." I swing my feet to the floor. Where the hell are my pants?

"Where are you going?"

"Home. The kids shouldn't find me here."

Ian sighs and gets out of bed. "Don't go anywhere yet. I'll be right out." He disappears into the bathroom while I hunt around for my clothes, and by the time he comes out, I'm dressed again, sitting on the foot of the bed.

"I'll sleep on the couch," he says, apparently unperturbed at being naked in front of me. "I'm just going to grab a shower first."

I stare at the floor. "I prefer to go home."

"Why? It's nearly morning anyway."

"Exactly. I have to get up for work soon."

He's silent for a moment. "Okay. Suit yourself."

"Do you have a sitter for tomorrow night—tonight—Jesus, I don't even know what day it is."

"Told you I could make you forget that."

I look over at him, careful to keep my eyes on his smug expression and not let them drift lower. "You did. Congratulations." I stand up. "But what I didn't forget was who you are and who I am and all the reasons why you and I do not belong together."

"Jesus, London. It was just sex."

Just sex. Right.

"Did you not want it?" he asks when I remain silent.

"I wanted it." I refuse to let him make me a victim.

He shrugs. "So did I. So there you go. Two consenting adults had some sex, and it was a good time. No one died. The end."

It's so easy for him to dismiss it that way. I have to remember that next time he comes at me with those hands and that mouth and the big, stupid, magical dick. Because it's not easy for me, and if I'm not careful, those feelings I've worked so hard to keep buried all these years will come rushing to the surface.

"You're right," I say. "And now that it's out of our system, we can move on. See you Saturday. If the kids need anything before then, let me know."

I congratulate myself on not eyeballing his junk as I walk by him and head down the hall. See? I can be strong. I can get past this. I can totally be the kind of woman who enjoys sex with a guy she hates because dammit, the chemistry is good. I grab my purse off the kitchen table and let myself out the back door.

Once, I clarify to myself as I hurry across Ian's yard and into mine. I can enjoy it once. Moving forward, it's out of the question.

I let myself in the back door of my house, and immediately my cat comes looking for attention, meowing and curling around my legs. Bending down, I give him some love before I head upstairs to my bathroom. It's only five-thirty, and I normally don't get up for another hour, but something tells me I wouldn't be able to sleep anyway.

Instead, I get into my shower and stand beneath the spray, picturing Ian doing the same.

Asshole.

The water drips down, washing away what just happened. I feel dirty, used, and yet I keep hearing myself begging him to go further, deeper, harder. There was no denying how much I wanted him. The feel of his hands on my body was everything I remembered and more.

But I'm a total idiot if I think there won't be any fallout after what just happened.

God, I could use a phone call with Sabrina right now.

Once I'm all clean, I get dressed and head out to the deck with my coffee. I look at his house, wondering what he's doing and if he feels half as conflicted as I do.

I curl up on the outdoor couch, pulling the blanket snugly around me, and lean my head back.

Next thing I know, I hear screaming and jolt off the couch.

"Chris! Give it back!" Morgan screams.

Shit. I fell asleep.

"Say you're sorry!" Christopher yells back at her, holding her backpack over the pool.

"No!"

"I'll drop it!"

Morgan tries to grab at it.

"Christopher!" I yell his name, but before he can respond, Ian exits the house.

Ruby is on his hip, and he marches right towards his nephew. Ian rips the backpack out of Christopher's hands, tosses it to Morgan, and then shoves Chris in the pool.

"Ian!" I call out without thinking.

Our eyes meet across the yard and my stomach drops. He looks angry. Really fucking angry. He also doesn't have a shirt on and looks ridiculously hot.

Great. I need this like a hole in the head.

I lift my hand tentatively, not wanting to be un-neighborly after fucking each other's brains out.

Does the bastard wave back?

Nope.

He flips me off like the immature jackass he is.

"Real nice, Ian." I lift my mug instead of the finger I'd like to send his way. "I'm glad to see you have the morning routine down pat! You're doing great there, huh?"

He shakes his head and walks back inside his fortress.

I stand here for a second, fighting back the urge to march over there and beat some sense into him. How dare he treat me like I'm the bad guy? I didn't crawl on top of him. I didn't lie in his bed and give him any indication that I wanted to have sex.

I was just fine on the damn couch.

He picked me up.

He carried me.

He touched me, made me beg for his cock, and then I begged for it...

Ugh.

I head inside, slamming the door behind me. Only that man can make me this angry. I swear, I'm the most even-tempered and level-headed person unless I'm around Ian Chase.

Thankfully my impromptu nap didn't set me too far off my schedule. Showering and getting dressed earlier actually saved me the eighteen minutes I slept over. I grab my pre-made overnight oats from the fridge and head out the door for a long day at the office.

Where my life is put together and the only complication is how much of a raise I should get for being such a badass.

~

"I understand that, Casey, but I can't travel this weekend," I try to explain to my boss.

There's no way I can bail on Ian tomorrow. He'll never find a sitter in time, and I can't do that. No matter the very undefined status of our—whatever we want to call it—it wouldn't be fair to him.

I agreed to care for the kids at night on our designated days, and I don't break my word. But I don't want to tell my boss that. He won't give a crap about my plight, and he might doubt my ability to handle bigger accounts if I indicate I have a higher priority than work right now.

As if on cue, Casey continues, "You're single, no kids, and the client that we've been vetting for six months wants you to go to New Jersey. There are no options here."

"I can't go tonight, I just can't."

He huffs. "You better have an amazing reason why not."

My anger starts to build as he waits for my reason, but I don't owe him one. I can't go and that should be enough. "I don't have to give you a reason. Per my contract, I require forty-eight hours' notice for any travel. This is less than twenty-four."

"This is a million-dollar account, London," he growls.

In other words, this is your job and I don't give a shit about your contract.

Dammit.

"Let me see what I can do," I sigh.

"You have an hour. Figure out whatever you need to, but make it happen." He pauses at the door and turns back. "The position for the Vegas supervisor is opening up soon, London. We both know you're the obvious choice, but something like this could really sway me towards Martin. I would think hard about whatever is keeping you back..."

"I understand."

When he closes my door, I drop my head on my desk. Could this day get any worse? It's just one damn thing after another. This is the job I've been working my ass off for every day for years. Moving up in this company is difficult, and I've done everything to get to this point.

Ugh.

I need to talk to Ian and figure a way out of this. I grab my phone and make the call I know is going to go over like a brick through glass.

"Hello." Ian's sleepy voice fills the line.

"Shit, sorry, I'll call back," I whisper. "I didn't mean to wake you."

I forgot he didn't get home till three-thirty and then he used his big magical dick to make me do things under duress.

I hear movement through the phone. "It's fine. I'm up now. What's wrong?"

Okay. I need to take advantage of his hopefully hazy-bad-decision-making wakeup. "Nothing's wrong, I just have a problem."

Ian groans. "So something is wrong if you have a problem."

"Right." This is going so well. "I have to go out of town..."

Silence.

"Ian?" I prompt.

"When?"

"Umm, I have to fly out late tonight... It was totally unexpected, and my boss is being really rigid on it. I tried so hard to get out of this, but I've been trying to land this account for a year. It's... it's just not something I can say no to, but I don't want to let you down either," I ramble as fast as I can before his wrath is sure to come.

And I wait.

And wait.

However, the only thing that happens is complete and total silence.

I bite my lip, and nerves flutter in my stomach as the quiet speaks loudly. Did he hang up? Is he so mad he isn't even going to respond?

I look down at the screen to check, but the time is still going.

Well, this awkward.

"You're running away," he finally says.

"What?"

"You're running away. We have sex and now you suddenly need to leave town on the day you say you'll watch the kids."

He's got it all wrong. "I'm not running anywhere and this has nothing to do with what happened this morning. This has to do with my job. I don't have a choice, Ian."

I know Ian lives in the world where everything revolves

around him, but this isn't fair. I love those kids and I just fought with Casey about going in the first place.

"Whatever," he huffs.

"You're such a dick. I didn't want to have to call you. I didn't want to do this, but I have a job too, you know?"

"Do whatever you need to, London, just like I will."

"What does that mean?"

"Nothing. Can I go back to bed now or do you want to tell me you're moving and I need to get a live-in nanny since you're unreliable already?"

So he's going to punish me for needing to work? He's acting as though I enjoy going back on my word.

"I'm sure one of your conquests would be up for the job," I say, letting my anger come through.

Ian lets out a laugh and then goes quiet.

"What's so funny?"

"Nothing, just that I thought I already had that. But seems the women I fuck aren't able to hold up their end of the bargain. Or maybe it's just the one I fucked last night."

The air vanishes from my lungs and it feels like I've been punched. I can't say anything because words fail me. I knew what happened last night meant nothing and that I left, but his words were cruel. Tears prick my eyes, but I hold them back.

"Yeah, seems we both had misconceptions about the other person. Thanks for the reminder, Ian."

I hang up the phone, and a tear falls.

CHAPTER TWELVE

ian

I'm a fucking asshole.

I know this.

When she left this morning, it was like being thrown back in the past all over again. She left without a backward glance. She acted like she wasn't a willing participant and I was just a guy who needed to get laid.

She didn't see how bad I wanted her.

How, as much as I want to hate her, I looked at her like she was the fucking sun in the sky.

She called it a mistake and walked out.

After she left, I took my shower, drank a shit ton of coffee, and stared at her backyard. I stood at the window, watching her long, wet brown hair brush against her back as she moved toward the couch on her deck. Watched how she pulled the blanket around her. Wished it was my arms holding her close.

Then I remembered her words. *"But what I didn't forget was who you are and who I am and all the reasons why you and I do not belong together."*

Who I am.

Fuck her and her goddamn self-righteousness. She's not better than me.

I was starting to get through my anger and then the kids got up. After that I went from pissed off to the verge of losing my fucking mind. This morning was like an episode of Married . . . with Children mixed with Shameless, and throw in a little Family Guy for the hell of it.

No one listened to a damn word I said.

It was complete chaos and I'm not even sure I dropped them off at the right places.

I throw the phone across the room, pissed at her, myself, and everyone I haven't spoken to yet.

Then the damn thing rings again just to mock me.

Great. It's my mother. This should be fun.

"Hello, Mom," I say, trying to calm myself down.

"Hi, honey. How are things going?"

"Just great."

If you consider tossing my nephew into the pool because punching him wasn't the better option great, then I'm telling the truth.

"Kids are good?"

"They're alive, let's just be happy about that."

My mother was Betty-fucking-Crocker. She baked us cookies while dad mowed the yard. She had the perfect house with the white picket fence and a boy and a girl. It was the textbook family life that everyone wanted. I don't think I can recall one time she raised her voice—she didn't have to. Dad was the enforcer and he was scary as fuck. Mom simply pointed with her lips tight or said, "don't make me tell your father," and we were perfect angels.

If she had seen the shit show that existed here a few hours ago, she'd have my father beat me.

"Ian, you need to rely on London if it's too much."

My mother would've sold me to get her. I swear, she likes her more than me. "I am. Your perfect adopted daughter just bailed on me instead of watching the kids."

"She wouldn't do that if she could avoid it," she says, defensive.

"Well, she did."

"What did you do to her then?"

"What did I—?"

She cuts me off. "Yes, you know that London has been in love with you since you were kids."

"Mom, you don't know what you're talking about."

"Do you think I'm an idiot? Something happened between the two of you before she left for college, and I'm sure it wasn't anything to be proud of, son."

Once again, I'm the bad guy. "You know, what if it was her that broke my heart? Huh?"

"Don't be silly," she laughs.

She did break my fucking heart. She made me break my own, that's what she did. I was head over heels in love with that girl. I was just waiting for the perfect chance to touch her, kiss her, love her, and then I got it only to have to walk away.

No one sees that, though.

"I need to get some sleep, Mom. The kids are fine, adjusting, as we all are. I need to find someone to watch them tonight and now over the weekend, since London has other shit she needs to do."

"I wish I could help."

I wish she could too. Mom would've had these kids off to school with lunches made and a three-course breakfast in their stomachs. I sent them with Pop-Tarts and a few bucks to buy lunch. I'm just impressed I remembered to give them cash at this point.

"I'll talk to you soon."

She sighs. "Okay, honey, have them call me today so we can chat."

"I will."

"And don't forget to call a real estate agent about the house. That needs to go on the market."

Oh, shit. I forgot about the house. "Hey, Mom, do you think

you could maybe do that? I've really got my hands full with the kids."

She sighs heavily. "I knew I should have stayed there. Do you want me to come back?"

"No!" The last thing I need is two women who think I'm a useless dickhead up in my face all the time. "No need for that. If you could just make the phone call, that would be great."

She sighs heavily. "Fine, I'll take care of the house. You stay focused on the children, and don't shut London out when she tries to help."

"Thanks for calling. Bye, Mom." I flop back down on my bed, and catch a whiff of London's perfume. I roll over onto my stomach, inhaling everything that is her.

How can you hate someone so much and yet want them at the same time?

She frustrates the fuck out of me, and all I want is to bury my dick inside her right now.

Memories flash through my mind of how unbelievable this morning was. How perfectly I fit inside her. How she moaned my name, clenching her pussy so tight around me I thought I'd die from how good it felt.

Great, I'm fucking hard now.

The doorbell rings, since I'm apparently never allowed to sleep again.

I trudge to the door still semi-hard, but it's nothing my housekeeper hasn't seen before. Jeanette has been with me for nine years. She was my housekeeper when I was married to the cunt, Jolene, and I took her with me. She's cleaned up more than her fair share, but she loves me unconditionally. Unlike the other women in my life.

"Jean—" I start to say with a smile, but the smile falls when I see who it really is.

"You have some nerve!" London glares as she pushes against my chest. "You think you can just say whatever you want to hurt me? You think you're so much better than me? Huh?"

"Why don't you come in?" I ask sarcastically as I close the door behind her.

"Fuck you and your asshole comments. I'm so tired of it. I'm not running anywhere. You want to talk, then be an adult and talk!"

"I don't want to talk," I say, moving toward her. "I don't want to say a fucking word to you. You said it all this morning."

She huffs and tosses her purse on the hall table. "What? What did I say that has you so pissed off that you treat me as though I'm just some insignificant slut in your life?"

It's not what she says, it's what she doesn't say. I've had it with this shit. I thought if we kept it buried, it would die, but it seems I was wrong.

"I think you've got this all wrong, sweetheart." I get closer to her, my fingers just grazing her wrist. "I never treated you like that. You're the one who called it sex and left. You're the one that said we weren't good together."

Her breath hitches and she steps back. "No, we're not doing this again. You're not going to use your charm on me this time. I'm wide awake now and we're going to talk about everything!"

She thinks I'm charming. That's what I heard at least. And all her mouth does is get me hard. Her anger makes me want to lay her down and shut her up in a million ways. It's like foreplay for us, and now that I've had her, I want her again.

"Fine, strip then."

"What?" she screeches.

"You want to talk, take your shirt off."

"You're insane!"

"Maybe, but if you want to talk, I want you vulnerable and unable to run away."

Total bullshit. I want her naked so I can see every inch of her again.

"No!"

"If you want to talk, I want insurance you're not going out

that door at the first thing I say that you don't like. So, take your fucking clothes off or go. You pick."

She puts her hands in her hair. "God, you are such a fucking jerk. It's unbelievable."

But what's really unbelievable is that her fingers move to the buttons of her burgundy silk blouse and start undoing them one by one, starting from the top. After about six of them, she stops. Her blouse is open now, still tucked into her black pencil skirt, and I'm fucking riveted by the sight of the nude lace bra she's wearing. I bet I'll be able to see her nipples right through it. My dick jumps around in my pajama pants.

She parks a hand on her hip and looks directly at my crotch. "Nice."

"Thank you." I adjust myself. "Now keep going. All the way off."

Her eyes narrow, and for a moment I think she's just going to storm out and I'll be stuck here alone with my hard-on. But she doesn't—she can't resist a fight either. She pulls the blouse from her skirt and finishes the task so it hangs open. "Happy?"

"It's a start. Now the skirt."

She glares at me like she wants to take off one of her sky-high heels and stab me with it. "You're despicable."

"You're a chicken."

Her jaw drops. "What?"

"You heard me. You're scared to have this conversation, so you're keeping all your high and mighty armor on." I make chicken noises at her like a fucking fifth grader.

She unzips her skirt and it falls to the floor. Stepping out of it, she brushes it aside with one high-heeled foot and sticks her hands on her hips again. "There. Now that you can clearly see I'm not going to run away, what is it you want to talk about?"

To be honest, I can't remember shit about what I wanted to say right now. I can see her raspberry-colored nipples through the nude lace of her bra, and the matching panties don't hide much either.

I take a step toward her and she backs up against the front door. Puts her hands out.

"Stop right there. Don't come any closer."

"Why not?" I move so close her palms are on my chest.

"You said we were going to talk, Ian."

I cage her in with my arms on either side of her, bracing my hands against the door. "Is that really what you want to do right now?"

"Yes," she snaps. But her breath is coming harder and faster, her breasts rising and falling with it.

"Okay." I stare down at her. "Talk. Tell me all the reasons you can't stand me. Tell me again how I broke your heart. Tell me we're no good together."

Her eyes meet mine. "You treat me like a plaything. You don't respect me. You make me feel bad about myself."

"How about I make you feel good right now? Would that help?"

"No." She pushes me away slightly. "I don't even understand why you want to."

"Yes, you do."

Our eyes are locked in a fiery stare. "Fine," she admits. "But just because the sex is good doesn't mean—"

"It's better than good and you know it."

She bites her plush bottom lip. I want to bite it too.

"You can't stand me, either," she says, but her tone is weakening, like this is her last line of defense, and her eyes have started to wander over my shoulders, chest and abs.

"Most of the time, that's true," I tell her. "You can be a cold, condescending bitch."

"I have to be, Ian." Her hands are moving now, sliding down my chest. "It's how I protect myself from you."

I lower my mouth to her neck, and she tilts her head to allow me to brush my lips against the side of her throat. "Lower your guard, London. You don't need to protect yourself from me anymore."

"Lies," she says as I kiss her neck. "You say these things, but you don't mean them. It's all a game with you." Her hands have reached the drawstring of my pants, which hang low on my hips. Her fingers hesitate.

"Go on." I whisper the words in her ear. "Do it."

"If I do, things change from this point forward."

Oh fuck, she's going to make demands now? When she's got me this hard for her? This weak for her? This desperate to get inside her again? "Yes. Whatever you want."

She unties the string and my pants fall to the floor. In an instant her hand is wrapped around my erection and my mouth is closing over hers.

Things escalate quickly from there.

My hands beneath her thighs. Her legs around my waist. My fingers tugging lace aside. Her back against the door. My cock moving inside her, hot and hard and fast, while her hands twist into my hair, fisting tight.

Our sounds bounce off the floor tiles and echo throughout the two-story foyer. Her gasps and cries. My groans and growls. The door rattling in its frame. Or maybe it's the entire house shaking—it is, it's a fucking earthquake, it has to be. There's no other explanation for the way the floor is vibrating beneath my feet. The hot, humming sensation moves up my legs, gathering strength, and I fuck her so violently I'm sure the entire front wall of the house is going to give and we'll tumble onto the front lawn.

She comes first, screaming my name before sinking her teeth into my shoulder as her body clenches mine. The sting of her bite only heightens the pleasure for me, and I erupt inside her in a series of powerful bursts, my entire body trembling with the force of it.

Afterward, my legs nearly give out, and I have to take a moment to let my muscles recover and regain some strength. We're both breathing hard, and her forehead is resting on my shoulder. It's kind of nice, and for a moment I wonder what it would be like if the next words out of her mouth were something sexy or affectionate and not defensive or bossy.

But I know her too well. She doesn't want me to know how much I get to her.

Sure enough, she doesn't disappoint.

Her head pops up. "Let me down."

Carefully, I disengage from her body and set her on her feet. She's still wearing her lingerie and heels, which is hot as fuck. But why does she have to wear that furrowed-brow expression too? She's looking at me like I'm a fly in the fruit salad, not like I just gave her an orgasm so intense she bit me.

"I'll be right back," she says, her heels clicking on the tile as she walks away from me. A moment later, I hear the bathroom door close.

"Fuck." I run a hand through my hair. We didn't use a condom—I always used a condom. Never, not once in the twenty years I'd been having sex had I ever been tempted to fuck someone without one. Jolene wouldn't even let me near her without one, she was so worried about getting pregnant and tipping the scale one ounce above her ideal body weight. But just now with London, it hadn't even occurred to me to stop and go get one. What the hell was I thinking?

Now she's going to come out here squawking about diseases and risks and how we both have to go get tested. Well, I get tested often enough that I have results from a month ago, and I haven't been with anyone since then but her. And fuck her if she doesn't believe me!

Angrily, I pull on my pants and tie the drawstring. When I hear the bathroom door open, I widen my stance and hoist up my chest a little, preparing for the fight.

But when she comes around the corner into the front hall, she doesn't look too battle-ready. She looks sort of sad and vulnerable. With her eyes on the floor, carrying her heels, she walks barefoot over to her skirt and blouse, scooping them up. Then she turns to me. "We should talk, don't you think?"

I'm so thrown by the change in her demeanor, I can't think. "Okay."

"Give me a minute to get dressed." Her eyes meet mine, and they're not accusatory or cold. They're soft. Her voice is soft, too. "I promise I will not run away. I just want to put my clothes back on."

"That's fine," I say, unsure how to tread these unfamiliar waters. "You can use my room."

"Thanks."

I follow her to the kitchen, where she turns down the hallway to my room. Seeing her walk that way, with her head down, her shoulders rounded, arms clutching her clothes, sort of makes me feel bad that I just banged her against the front door. What kind of animal am I?

Frowning, I turn on the Keurig, grab a coffee pod from the pantry, and stick it in. While I wait for it to brew, I lean back against the counter and rub my face with both hands. More than anything, I wish Sabrina was around so I could ask for advice. I don't understand London at all. There's obviously still something between us, and it could be good, but we insist on fighting each other. Why? Is it our history? Do I need to come clean about what I did?

Back when it all went down, I planned on telling her the truth eventually. But I needed her to take that scholarship and go away to school first. I figured I'd tell her when she graduated. I never dreamed she'd still be so mad she'd refuse to even talk to me. When they say hell hath no fury like a woman scorned, let me assure you, they are not kidding. London wouldn't even be in the same room with me for a while, and when she was, her eyes were like knives on my skin.

At that point I figured, fuck her. She didn't want to hear me out? Fine. She didn't want to know I'd only done it for her? Fine. She didn't want to hear me say she was the only girl I'd ever loved and wanted to give us another chance? Fine. It wasn't like I'd be lonely.

From then on, it was war between us.

But now that Sabrina's death has thrown us together, I find myself wishing things could change. I don't even know what I want exactly, but when I hear the bedroom door open and bare feet coming down the hall, I make up my mind to try harder not to be an asshole, even if she picks a fight.

She appears in the kitchen, carrying her shoes in one hand. My heart beats faster at the sight of her—she's redone her hair, pulling it back off her face so her green eyes look huge and luminous. Her cheeks are flushed, and her lips look a little swollen. She's as beautiful as she was at seventeen—more, even.

"Do you want some coffee?" I ask.

"Sure." She sets her shoes down next to the island.

"What flavor?" I go into the pantry and look in the sampler box. "My housekeeper buys all kinds of them. I've got French vanilla, hazelnut, butter toffee, Krispy Kreme—"

"French vanilla is fine."

"Regular or decaf?"

"Regular."

"You got it." I grab it from the box and exit the pantry. She's still standing across the kitchen from me, holding one elbow, one bare foot covering the other.

When I pull out the pod I used, I saw that I made for myself exactly what she chose. "Here. You can have this one." Feeling magnanimous, I take the full, steaming cup from the machine and set it next to her on the island.

"Are you sure?"

"Positive." I start brewing the second cup and turn around to face her. "So."

"So."

We stand there staring at each other for a moment. "You came over to talk?"

She nods. "Yes."

I fold my arms over my chest and lean back against the counter. "What about? The weekend travel thing? Because we can work that out. I'm sorry I blew up about that." Apologizing doesn't come easy for me, and she seems to know it judging by the stunned expression on her face.

"Oh." She blinks a couple times. "Well, good. Thank you. That makes my life a lot easier."

Damn, I feel like a god. "Great."

"But it's more than the travel thing."

"Okay."

Her eyes drop to the coffee cup, which she takes in her hands without lifting from the counter. "What did you mean when you said I was running away?"

Oh, fuck. I did say that, didn't I? "Uh . . . I'm not sure what I meant."

She looks up at me. "Can we please be honest with each other for once? No games?"

I swallow hard. Then I nod. "Okay. I said that because I thought what we did last night scared you, and you wanted to run away rather than admit it."

"Is that why you made me take off my clothes when I got here? Because you thought I'd run away again?"

I hesitated. "Honestly? No. I just wanted to see you naked again."

She rolls her eyes. "I knew it."

"But I am curious. Did last night scare you?"

"Yes."

"Why?"

"Because . . ." She stares down at the coffee again.

"Come on, you have to be honest now, too."

"Because you scare me, Ian. I have—conflicting feelings about you. I always have."

"Well, you'll be glad to know we're in the same boat." I turn to reach for my coffee. When I face her again, she's staring at me, wide-eyed.

"You have feelings?"

I slay her with a look. "Hey. We're having a nice talk. Don't ruin it."

She holds up both hands. "Sorry, that came out wrong. I meant, you have *feelings* feelings for me? Because that's what I have for you. At least sometimes."

"Yes, London. I have *feelings* feelings for you. Sometimes. When you're not calling me names or ordering me around." I sip my coffee as if this is a casual conversation and I'm totally calm, but my stomach is in knots. Talking this way, being so candid with her, is really fucking strange. But I like it, sort of. At least, I like the way it's got her so off guard. She looks like she doesn't even know what to do with herself.

"Wow. I'm . . . I wasn't expecting you to say that."

"Then I guess you're not expecting me to ask you on a date, either."

Her jaw drops. "A date?"

"Yes, a date. You know—a boy-girl, drive-in movie, steam-up-the-windows kind of thing." The date idea came out of nowhere, but now I'm into it.

Eyes closed, she shakes her head as if to clear it from confusion. "Am I in the right house?"

I grin at her and take another sip of coffee. "How about one day next week when you get back from your trip?"

"Ian, why do you want to take me on a date? It's not that I don't want to go, it's just that I want to make sure I understand what this is."

"What do you think it is?"

"I thought it was just sex, and just for fun. That's what you said this morning."

"I meant, It's just sex, there is no reason to freak out. Not, It's just sex and nothing more. You were the one who called it a mistake before we even got out of bed."

"Because I thought I was just another notch in your bedpost," she blurts. "I figured you were just scratching an itch."

"Scratching an itch?" I set my cup down and cross my arms again. "Did you think I used you for sex?"

"Kind of."

I have to laugh. "London, if I was just looking for sex, I wouldn't have come to you. There are plenty of women who'd—"

She puts out a hand. "Okay, enough. You can just stop that sentence there, I don't need to hear the end of it."

"Sorry." I moved toward her. "But if that's what had you all worked up, you can relax." Taking her by the shoulders, I turn her to face me, set my hips against hers. "I want more. How much more, I'll be honest and say I don't know, but not just sex."

She can't keep a smile from forming, or the blush from her cheeks. "Really?"

"Really." I press my lips to hers, and it's a different kind of kiss than we've had so far, one not inspired by frustration or impatience or lust. Instead, this one is about honesty. Affection. *Feelings* feelings.

Jesus. I hope I can handle this.

CHAPTER THIRTEEN
London

I'm living in an alternate reality. That's the only thing that can explain this. Ian... wants to go... on a date... with me? Not possible.

Yet I was standing right there. I heard the words, his lips were moving, and it happened.

I've been packing my suitcase for the last two hours because each time I think I'm done, I realize I only packed underwear or ten pairs of pants but no shirts.

I can't think straight and it's pissing me off.

All I want is to talk to my best friend, but I don't have that option anymore.

"Fuck this," I say to my cat as I dump my bag out on the bed. "I'm going to get answers so I can function."

He looks up at me and then lies back down. Helpful cat.

I grab my phone and send him a text.

Me: Did you mean it? About the date?

Ian: Yes.

Me: You're not just fucking with me as some sort of hazing experiment?

Ian: Are you drunk again?
Me: I'm not drunk.

I wish I was drunk. It would explain the conversation we had three hours ago. My flight leaves in a few hours and I shouldn't be worried about Ian and his sudden feelings.

Ian: Did you change your mind?

I look at the message, trying to figure out how to answer him. If I say I changed my mind, I'm lying because I don't know that I ever made up my mind, but more than that, I'm still . . . in shock. However, Ian put himself out there. He was kind, sweet even, after we had sex—again. It's unlike we've been towards each other for the last twenty years and it's confusing as hell.

Me: No. I just want to give you an out.

Yes, that's it. I want him to have the chance to say he was joking now, before my heart softens even the slightest bit. My emotions with Ian are a rubber band in so many ways. I stretch and stretch until I'm at the point of snapping, but if I eased the tension, I'd go right back to my original form.

I'm used to being stretched.

I almost prefer that because when I wasn't, I was head over heels in love with him.

If this goes bad, there's no doubt I'll break.

Ian: Good. Open your door.

Me: My door?

What the hell?

I walk down the stairs and do as he says.

When I open it, he's standing there shirtless with his shorts sitting low on his hips.

"Hey," I say.

Ian steps forward, grips my face in his hands, and kisses me.

I'm thrown so far off guard that I fall back a little, but he's got me. His lips mold to mine and I hold onto him for support. He cradles my cheeks in his hands, holding me right where he wants me. I can't think as he continues to kiss me.

I never want this to stop. Every woman should know what this kind of kiss feels like. The passion right now is so overwhelming, I could drown in it.

After God only knows how long, he leans back, pressing our foreheads together.

"I've wanted to kiss you like that for a long time," he says as I try to calm my racing heart. "I'm not changing my mind. I want us to go out and have fun, and then I'm going to kiss you on your doorstep and walk to my house thinking about how much I want you. I'll wonder if you're in your bed, thinking about me and wishing you were back in my bed. I've spent a long time trying to hate you, London, but the truth is I never really did. So." He leans back and our eyes meet. "Have a safe trip and I'll see you when you get back."

My lips part and I stand there at a total loss for words. Is this the same Ian I've spent my entire adult life hating, yet somehow knowing it was just because in the depths of my heart I still loved him?

He kisses my cheek and walks out the door, leaving me a mess.

I blink a few times, waiting for the dream to end, to wake up, but nothing changes. Holy fucking shit, this day just keeps getting weirder.

Somehow, I make it back to my room, where all the contents of my suitcase are strewn across the bed.

Fuck it. I'll just buy clothes in New Jersey. There's no way I can pack now.

~

"I'm really glad you came out, London. This meeting was everything we hoped for. It's why we went with your company."

It's been non-stop meetings in Atlantic City. I have never been so physically and emotionally exhausted.

"Thank you for having me out and for taking such good care of me. I look forward to working with you and getting the proposal to you by next week." I smile warmly.

Right now, I don't even know what I'd analyze because I'm beat. I barely slept, even though the owner of the casino put me up in his penthouse suite and I was more than comfortable. Sure, I could try to blame the time change, but that would be a lie. It was all because when I closed my eyes, all I saw was Ian. Everything reminded me of him, the night we spent together, the kids, or the things he said before I left.

"Good. We'll talk soon, have a safe trip back home."

"Thanks again."

I get into the black sedan to head back to the airport. Back to the kids and Ian.

It's strange how in just a few short weeks my entire life has been altered. Things were so simple before. I wouldn't have hesitated to take this trip because I had nothing keeping me in Vegas. Sabrina wasn't impacted by my work life and she was really all I had.

Now, it's the kids and Ian. I spent the entire trip messaging them, trying to make sure everyone was okay and didn't need anything.

Ian ended up taking the kids to the club Friday night, which I am still not even a little bit okay with, but they left before the doors opened. Yesterday, he had his manager come stay at the house for a few hours when he went in. He didn't tell me this, but Morgan sure did.

I plan to talk to him about that.

The drive to the airport is long, and I end up taking a nap. Once I get to the airport, check in, and arrive at my gate, the flight is boarding. I pull out my phone, remembering that he sent me a text I never responded to.

Ian: What time do you land?

Me: I get in around two. I'll be there to watch the kids tonight, don't worry. I took off the next few days since I need to work on a proposal.

Then I shoot a message to Morgan.

Me: Did you get your project done or do we need to work on it when I get home?

Morgan: It's done, Uncle Ian helped. Well, kind of.

Oh, God. I was good up until the 'kind of.'

Ian: I'm not worried, but thanks. What airline are you flying?

I send him the screenshot of my flight info so he knows what time to expect me. I'll have plenty of time to get home, showered, and ready before he needs to leave. The flight attendant comes over the speaker, informing us we have to power down.

Me: Flight is taking off now. I'll see you later.
  Ian: See you soon.

Yeah, you will, and I pray to God you and I haven't lost our minds.

~

"Thank you for flying with us." The flight attendant smiles as I deplane.

"Sure." I smile back but don't mean it.

The flight was awful.

Turbulence was out of control, some kid was kicking my seat, even though I was in first class, and I couldn't get the Wi-Fi to work.

Seriously, worst flight ever. Well, maybe not the worst flight, because it actually landed. But it still sucked.

I start the long walk down the terminal to head to the car service that's waiting. I'm ready for a bath.

Two soldiers are practically running toward people holding signs with balloons, and I smile. My father served in the Army before he and my mother had me. There used to be a large photograph in our hallway of him returning from deployment. In the picture, my mother has her arms wrapped around his neck, holding his hat in her hands, and my father's smile is blinding. He didn't take it down even after she left us, and I always loved looking at it.

You could see in that moment how they both were just able to breathe again.

I've longed for that. The way he looked at her. The way she needed him. I want to feel that as well.

Even if it doesn't last.

"Aunt London!" I hear a voice I recognize yelling my name.

I shade my eyes, look for the source, and find Ruby waving frantically on the sidewalk coming toward me.

There, behind her, is Ian with a bouquet of roses, and Morgan and Christopher too.

"You guys." I make my way over, smiling. "What are you doing here?"

Morgan nudges her uncle. "Well, someone wanted to surprise you... because he likes you."

"You're grounded." Ian nudges her back.

"Why? Because I'm telling you the truth? You like her."

"You don't need to tell her that!"

Morgan rolls her eyes like the teenager she almost is. "No, it's much better to lie. And you're our role model?"

"This is why Ruby is my favorite," Ian says as he hoists the little peanut in his arms.

God, I've missed them.

"You did this?" I ask him, trying to save him from Morgan's pestering.

"I did. Are you surprised?"

I nod. "This is a great surprise."

I have the greatest urge right now to kiss him. He did something so sweet, knocking me on my ass again.

"Good. There's more."

"More what?"

Ruby smiles. "More fun!"

Well, this is interesting.

"Don't get too excited, Aunt London." Christopher shakes his head. "I wanted to go skydiving, but they had other ideas."

I laugh. "Well, I'm glad for that because you know I hate heights."

Ian sets Ruby down. "Let's get going so we can show her our plan. I have a feeling she's going to like it."

Ruby takes my hand. "I missed you."

"I missed you, too. Were you a good girl for Uncle Ian?"

She nods.

"Did you guys eat while I was gone?"

"Hey," Ian cuts in. "I fed them, made them do homework, and no one got injured. Which is more than I can say when you were around."

I laugh. "So you were able to act like an adult?"

"All by myself."

Then, Ian does something that completely takes me off guard. He wraps his arms around me, pulling me to his solid chest. My heart begins to race as his one hand glides up my back, securing me to him.

"Ian," I breathe. "The kids."

"I don't give a shit," he mutters.

"They..."

"Shut up, London, and let me kiss you."

I don't say a word because before I can even try, his lips press against mine. It's one of those head-spinning kisses too. Where the world fades away around us, and even surrounded at the airport, all that exists is Ian.

He does this to me, which is the scary part.

Morgan giggles and Christopher lets out a whistle. Ian and I break apart and my face is hot from embarrassment.

"That is how you kiss a girl." Ian nods once at Christopher.

Oh, dear God. "Please don't listen to a single thing your uncle says about dating. He's really very bad at it, and his learning curve is not a path you want to follow."

"What?" Ian is outraged.

"Seriously," Morgan agrees. "Remember Mom always said Uncle Ian needed a whole lot of help when it came to girls? I think she was right."

"Hey," he protests.

"What? You're kind of a mess." Morgan shrugs.

"You're kind of a pain in the ass. Anyone ever tell you that, kid?"

"Daily," Morgan says with pride.

At least she owns it. Morgan has always been an old soul. It's probably why I've always loved spending time with her, even when she was little. Christopher was always into sports and definitely related to David and Ian. They were always watching a game of some sort, while Morgan wanted to discuss the news. And she's a numbers girl, which is definitely something we share.

Ruby is the total dress-up girly-girl. I'm not sure how the hell I'll find a way to relate to her as she grows up. I don't care about designer clothes, jewelry, or makeup. I like nice things, but I've never been materialistic. Not that I think Ruby will always keep the same interests she has at five, but she loves to do things that Morgan never did.

"All right, enough about me, let's get going, we have a lot of ground to cover," Ian says.

Christopher grabs my bag, and we all start to walk. I place my hand on Ian's arm. "Thank you for this. It was really sweet."

He gives me one of his cocky grins. "I'm a sweet guy."

"You're something, all right."

"I promised you things would change. I thought a lot about you when you were gone, and I don't want things to go the way they have before, Lon."

"I don't either."

I want more. I want Ian and me to have a real shot at something, if it's possible. There's a deep history between us, but that's also the scary part. What if things don't work out? What do we do about the kids? I can't imagine my life without them in it, and he's their guardian. Do I think he'd keep them from me? No. But he could.

His hand cups my cheek. "I meant what I said before you left. You might think I've charmed you before, but you haven't seen anything yet. I hope you're ready."

My throat goes dry at his promise. "What if I'm not?"

He smiles down at me. "Then you better find a way—and fast."

CHAPTER FOURTEEN

ian

My plan is simple. Get London to let her freaking steel walls down and see that I'm a good guy.

That's it.

How the fuck I plan to do that? Not a clue.

The entire weekend I tried to remember any stupid detail my sister had rambled on about when it came to London. Of course, I had purposely tuned out anyone talking when her name came up to avoid feelings I didn't want to feel, so I had to get creative.

Things London likes: cats, terrible music, numbers, boring shit about business, and sun. I see her sitting out on her deck all the time, a book in her hand, those long bare legs stretched out on a deck chair, her horrible 90s boy-band music playing. I swear to God, London has good taste when it comes to many things, but music is not one of them. She and Sabrina used to drive me crazy playing that shit twenty-four hours a day.

But today is all about getting her to see me in a new light, so I've loaded up a London Playlist with all kinds of crap by bands like N'Sync, Backstreet Boys, and Four Blocks Down. I'm going to indulge her in every way possible.

Even if my eardrums suffer for it. Mightily.

"This is all you have?" I ask her, reaching for the handle of her small black suitcase.

"Yes. I traveled light." She lowers her face to the roses and inhales, her eyes closing. "Thank you for this."

"You're welcome." I look at the kids, give Morgan a wink. "Should we go?"

The two girls shout "Yes!" and Christopher gives a nod. He's had a decent weekend so far, and we even had what I thought was a pretty good talk last night after I got home from the club. I can't wait to tell London about it.

"Where are we going?" asks London as we start heading toward the parking lot, Morgan and Christopher in the lead.

"It's a surprise." I take Ruby's other hand so she doesn't get lost in the crowd.

"Can I go home and clean up first?"

"We'll go by your house, and you'll have two minutes to run in and change."

"Into what?"

"A bathing suit."

She grins at me. "That's it?"

"That's it."

"Then two minutes is all I'll need. Maybe one more to feed Eli Walsh."

"Morgan and Ruby fed your cat this morning."

She smiles at Ruby. "Thanks, girls. How's he doing? Did he miss me?"

"No, because we went over and played with him a lot," Morgan says over her shoulder. "We didn't want him to be lonely without you, like Uncle Ian."

"Hey." I frown in my niece's direction, wishing I had a free hand to poke her. "I never said I was lonely."

"I asked you if you missed her and you said yes. That means you were lonely," she says sweetly, like duh.

London giggles. "She's poking all kinds of holes in your game, Ian. Pretty soon you'll have none left."

"Oh, I will always have game," I say confidently, sticking out my chest a little as we cross the street. It feels good to hear her laugh. It feels good to be getting along with her. It feels good to walk like this, Ruby between us, Morgan and Chris just ahead, almost like we're a family.

Somewhere, Sabrina is smiling. I know it.

~

True to her word, London is in and out of her house in two minutes, wearing a black cover-up, flip flops, a big straw hat, and carrying a beach bag.

She's a little breathless when she gets back in the car. "Whew. How'd I do?"

"Perfect."

She buckles her seatbelt and pulls a pair of sunglasses out of her bag. Slipping them on, she looks into the back of the minivan as I pull out of her driveway. "I brought a bunch of sunscreen, you guys. We need to make sure we get some on you if we're going to be outside."

"We already put it on, and we packed some," Morgan announces.

I can't help feeling triumphant when London looks at me, her mouth falling open.

"Who are you?" she asks. "And what have you done with the real Ian Chase?"

"Babe, I'm just getting started." Grinning, I glance at the dash and turn up the volume on the car stereo, which is already connected to my phone and playing one of her favorites, "Once in a Lifetime."

She gasps and stares at the radio like it's performing magic. Then she squeals like a teenager. "I love this song!"

"I know."

She starts singing along, fake mic and all, and I have to laugh because she has a horrible singing voice, but she does not care at all. Even the kids are groaning in the back, but London is in the zone.

"You're the only girl I see. I want to wake up next to you. Will you be my once in a lifetime?" she croons dramatically.

I wonder if my windshield will crack.

"Uncle Ian, is she going to do this all the way to Lake Mead?" Christopher asks.

London stops singing and straightens up in the seat. "Lake Mead?"

"We rented a boat!" cries Ruby.

"You guys, you weren't supposed to give it away," Morgan scolds.

"That's okay," I say quickly, catching Ruby's eye in the rearview mirror and giving her a wink. Her expression goes from worried back to joyful in a heartbeat. "It's not that long of a ride, so she'd probably guess it pretty soon."

London claps her hands. "I love Lake Mead! And I haven't been on a boat in forever. When I lived in Chicago, my roommate's family had a boat on Lake Michigan they kept at Belmont Harbor—well, it was fifty-five feet long, so it was more like a yacht—and I loved when they'd invite me out on it."

"Well, princess, I'm sorry to say, our boat today is only a twenty-two footer"—she reaches over and slaps my arm—"but it's perfect for waterskiing and tubing and knee boarding."

She bounces around in her seat. "Really? Oh my God, I haven't done any of that stuff in years! I'm not even sure I remember how."

"I'll teach you again." I glance at her, wondering if she remembers.

A smile curves her lips. "That's right. You taught Brina and me to water ski that summer your family got the place in Lake Tahoe. God, that was fun, wasn't it?"

"Yeah." For a moment, both of us get a little lost in the memory of that summer on the lake, when my sister was alive and life was uncomplicated, and our biggest problem was whether to kayak or windsurf each morning. "What was that, like twenty years ago?"

"Nineteen, I think. I remember I'd turned sixteen just before we went."

Morgan pipes up from the backseat. "Aunt London, what were you like when you were sixteen?"

"She was an annoying little pipsqueak just like your mother," I say with a grin. "Those two used to drive me crazy." Imitating their high-pitched teenaged voices, I go on. "Ian, will you take us out on the boat? Ian, can you teach us how to waterski? Ian, will you put the kayak in the water for us?"

London leans toward me and smacks the top of my thigh. "And your uncle here was a big meanie. He never wanted us around, but your grandma and grandpa said he had to put up with us."

"What was my mom like at sixteen?" Morgan asks.

My throat gets a little tight, so I'm glad when London answers the question, turning to face the back seat. "She was the best friend you could ask for. Outgoing, fun, always up for an adventure, always laughing, always sweet. Everyone loved her. And she was so loyal—she'd do anything for you. All you had to do was ask."

"Did she like this music too?"

"Oh, totally. We used to blast it in her bedroom and drive everyone in the house nuts. One time your uncle stole all your mom's CDs and hid them."

"True story," I say. "And I'm not sorry. You guys were obnoxious."

"What are CDs?" Ruby asks.

I groan as London bursts out laughing, touching my leg again. This time she leaves her hand there. "It's how we listened to music when we were young," she explains. Then she looks at me. "That means we're old, doesn't it?"

"Probably. But we don't have to act like it." When I glance at her, she has a sexy little smile on her face that makes the crotch of my shorts feel tight.

"No. We don't." She lets her fingers brush inappropriately close to my junk before pulling her hand away, and it's hard to keep a grin off my face.

I'm the happiest I've been in a long time.

∼

"Uncle Ian, do we have to go home?" Morgan is wrapped in her towel, her hair dripping, her nose and cheeks pink despite the sunscreen. "I don't want to."

"I'm afraid so. And we have to return the boat by seven, so we should probably start heading back."

Her face falls, and I don't blame her a bit. It's been a perfect afternoon—the weather hot and sunny, the water cool and refreshing, the kids laughing and enjoying themselves more than I've seen them do since losing their parents.

Even London is more relaxed than usual. She's a little rabid about the sunscreen, but it was kind of nice when she offered to put some on my back and shoulders. Her hands on my skin heated me up even more than the sun, and she pressed her lips to the back of my neck, prompting Morgan to taunt, "Are you guys in love or something?"

Rather than answer, I picked her up and tossed her over the side of the boat into the lake.

"Can I drive the boat back, Uncle Ian?" Christopher asks from where he's sitting with Ruby in the open bow.

I check my phone and see that it's already close to seven. Much as I don't want this day to end, I have to be at work by ten at the latest, and I still have to feed them dinner. "Sure. You guys ready to go? Do we have everyone on board?"

London, leaning back on her hands, legs outstretched across the cushion at the back of the boat, looks from kid to kid. "One, two, three. I think we're all here." Rising to her feet, she calls to

Ruby. "Come here, honey, and let's get your life jacket back on, okay? You too, Morgan and Chris." She smiles at the young girl and puts a hand beneath her chin. "God, you look just like your mom at your age with your hair all slicked back that way."

Morgan grins. "I do?"

London nods and gives her a hug, but I don't miss the sniff. She's wearing sunglasses, but I know if she took them off, I'd see tears in her eyes. Sabrina and David have been on my mind too today, and I like thinking that they're happy as they watch over us. I want their faith in me to be justified. It's becoming more important to me every day.

When all the kids have their life jackets on, we head back to the marina, turn in the boat, and pile into the car for the forty-five minute drive home. On the way, London offers to get the kids fed while I get ready for work.

"Thanks," I say, giving her a grateful smile. "That helps. I was just planning to order a pizza, but there are some things in the fridge if you feel like cooking."

"I'll make them something. I don't mind. They could probably use something healthy since they've been eating chips and drinking pop all day." She looks over at me says quickly, "I don't mean that as a criticism. I ate the chips, too."

Laughing, I reach over and squeeze her hand. "It's okay. Thanks for the help. And I promise I'm going to take you to dinner one night this week."

"That would be nice."

Back at my house, the kids tromp upstairs to shower and clean up, tired and cranky after a day in the sun. London heads for the kitchen, tosses her hat and sunglasses on the counter, and opens the fridge. "Oh, perfect," she says. "You've got chicken breasts and bell peppers. I'll make a stir fry. Do you have any rice?"

"Pantry, I think." I set my keys on the table.

"Great. I'm just going to run over to my house and grab a quick shower. Be right back." She tries to move past me but I catch her around the waist, wishing she didn't have to go, even for a quick shower.

"Hey," I say gruffly.

Smiling, she lets me pull her close. Her hands rest on my chest. "What?"

I kiss her softly. "Did you have a nice day?"

Her lips curve into a smile. "Yes. Did you?"

"Yes. I think the kids liked it too."

"I know they did. We should do things like this with them more often. Wasn't it wonderful to see them smiling like that? Especially Christopher."

"He and I had a nice talk last night."

Her eyebrows rise. "Did you? About what?"

"A lot of things. But mostly that it's okay for him to miss his parents. I told him how much I miss my sister, and I think he was glad to hear that."

Her eyes drop for a moment. "I think he really wants to be strong, but it's kind of an act, you know? And if he tries to bury all that pain..."

"That's probably my fault. When it first happened, I handled him like my father handled me all my life. Told him a man needs to hold it together, be brave for the women, not show weakness." I could tell she wanted to say something, but bit her lip instead. "But maybe that isn't the right approach with Chris. He seems a little more sensitive than I was at his age. More like his mom."

"I think you're right."

"Anyway, I think he felt better afterward."

She smiles. "Good job, Uncle Ian."

I close my eyes for a second. "But I still feel like I don't know what the fuck I'm doing."

"It's okay. You're doing great, and I'm here for you. We're a team. United front, remember?"

"I really want to make a joke about uniting fronts right now."

Laughing, she gently pushes me away and tries to get around me. "I have to go change or I'll never get out of this wet suit."

I catch her again from behind, wrapping my arms around her. "I could help with that."

"Ian, stop!" She giggles and attempts to pry my arms from her waist but they're locked tight. "You're going to be late for work."

"Fuck work." And I realize something—I don't even want to go to work. For the first time I can remember, I'd rather stay home and hang out with her and the kids than be at the club with its huge crowd and loud music and drunk girls falling all over me. What the actual fuck?

London stops moving. "Can you? I mean, do you have to go in?"

I exhale and drop a kiss on her shoulder. She smells like sunscreen and summertime. "Yeah, I do. But I'll get out of there as soon as I can. No pressure, but you're welcome to stay over. Wait —fuck that. Stay over."

She turns in my arms and looks up at me. "You want me to?"

"Yes. I might be late, but I've been thinking about you in my bed for two lonely nights. Stay."

Her eyes brighten and then she smiles. "Okay, I'll be here."

I lean down and kiss her, while my heart races.

Maybe we can actually make it work this time.

CHAPTER FIFTEEN
London

"Aunt London, are you going to marry Uncle Ian?" Ruby asks as I'm tucking her in.

Oh, Lord. This is the absolute last thing I want to talk about. "Umm." I cough and fidget with her stuffed panda. "Do you want me to read you a bedtime story?"

"Yes, please. The one about the princess and the frog."

Great. A fairytale about a frog turning into a prince. No symmetry there. "You've got it."

I lean over to the stack, fishing out the book she requested, grateful that five-year-olds are so easy to divert from the topic you want to avoid. She rests her head on my chest as I read, showing the photos as I go. We get to the end and she lets out a huge sigh. "Uncle Ian could be the prince and you can be the princess. You fall in love and get married, just like in the book."

Do I burst her bubble about her uncle? No, that would be cruel, but the woman in me can't let this opportunity pass. I hear Sabrina in my head about not ever needing a man, but having one because you want him.

"You know, a princess doesn't need a prince to be happy," I tell her as I kiss the top her head.

"Really?"

"Yup. In fact, some of the greatest women we know don't have a prince."

She scrunches her nose. "But Uncle Ian looks just like the prince did. And he took us on the boat."

Well, he looks better than the prince, but that's not the point. "Your uncle is pretty great, but I think the princess is happy because she found someone who was a good man and loved her for who she is."

Ruby yawns and moves to her pillow. "Okay. I still think you should be a princess and be happily after ever with Uncle Ian."

I giggle at her reversed words. "It's happily ever after."

"With Uncle Ian."

I'm totally not getting through to her.

"You never know," I say softly. My heart aches a little as I remember how I felt like that about him once before. Ian was the prince of my dreams. I would've done anything for him to love me.

"I love you, Auntie London."

I shake my head, pushing those thoughts from my head, and look back down at her. "I love you with my whole heart."

"And Uncle Ian too."

I laugh, knowing I'm totally going to lose this one to her. He's her hero and he should stay that way—always. "Goodnight, pipsqueak."

I tiptoe out of her room and check on the older kids. Chris is watching television and Morgan is creating the perfect Instagram photo, whatever that means. Much to my surprise, there's not much to do around here. The laundry is done, dishes are clean, and everyone is functioning.

Well, I guess I'll watch television . . .

My butt hits the couch and I realize how freaking exhausted I am. This weekend was crazy and I haven't slept at all. I lean my head back and try to absorb all that happened today. Ian was so sweet. He went above and beyond to do something nice for me, and I appreciated it, but it was nothing compared to him asking me to stay.

There's nothing on worth watching, so I grab my laptop from my bag beside me, and decide to do something to help me assemble my thoughts—I write. It's been a long time since I've journaled, but as soon as I open everything, I know who I want to write to and what I have to say.

I open my email, and begin to type.

Dear Sabrina,

You're gone. You're gone and my life isn't remotely the same. You gave Ian the kids, didn't see that one coming, but they're doing good. Thanks for the letter sort of explaining it. You really should've, you know, talked to me. I would've understood or at least bitched for a bit, tried to talk you out of it—okay, so maybe I do get why you didn't tell me.

Anyway, losing you has been hard on all of us. Ruby wouldn't speak —well, to anyone but me. Now, she's back to her bubbly self. Morgan is doing great, she's full of piss and vinegar. Chris had a hard time, but Ian helped him through.

Me? I'm struggling with everything, and I miss you. I want to open a bottle of wine and have you come over. I've been so alone since I lost you. So alone. Well, I guess I should say that I was. I felt like there was no way out of the pain of losing you, but then your stupid brother broke me down. I don't know how the hell it happened, but here I am, in his house, about to go to his bed.

Yup.

His freaking bed. As if the first go around didn't end in disaster, right? I know, I know, he's not the same kid he was. I hear you loud and freaking clear, but . . . he's . . . Ian. He's the guy that somehow always gets to me.

God, Sab, today he was that charming guy all over again. The guy who made my heart race and all I wanted was to be with him. I think I need to let go of all the past and forgive him. I should see him for who he is now, and that's the guy who, despite all my hate, has made me feel . . . different.

I'll say this to you because you're the only person I trust. I could fall in love with him so easily, but I won't. I can't, right? It would be stupid because we'll never work.

Okay, I lied to you and I can't do that. I'm going to fall in love with him because he's Ian and I've always loved him.

Damn it.

Oh, and since you'll never read this I can tell you all the details. We had sex. We had really, hot, sweaty, dirty sex. We did it in bed and then against the wall. Like, the sex you read about in the romance novels. Which I kept, by the way. I figure if you love that Jack Valentini guy so much, I'll read it and maybe torture Ian with how hot he is. We both know how much he loved it when you told him the stories.

I love you. I miss you. I think about you every day.

Love,

London

"Aunt London," Morgan's voice says in my ear.

Shit.

I close the laptop, hoping she didn't read over my shoulder. Especially since I wrote about dirty sex.

"Yes?"

"Is it true that boys are mean to you when they like you? I mean, we know Uncle Ian is mean to you because he's dumb, but are they all dumb?"

"Who's being mean to you?" I ask quickly, my hackles raised.

I'm not a mom but these tiny people are like my kids. I may not have birthed them but I've been around since their mom pushed them out. So, they're mine.

"No one." Morgan comes around and sits in front of me on the coffee table. "It's just this boy I like is always such a jerk. He makes fun of me sometimes, and then when his friends aren't around, he tells me I'm pretty."

Of all the people who she should ask for advice, I'm not the best choice. I'm sort of destined to be a spinster with a cat named after her favorite singer. My life choices regarding love haven't really been stellar.

"Have you asked your uncle or brother?"

"Gross. No."

I laugh. "Okay, well, they're both boys. They probably know a little more about this than me."

"They're dumb."

"This is true, but Morgan, your uncle was definitely mean to me and I think he likes me a lot."

Her smile grows and she scrunches her shoulder. "I know. It's so cute. He was stressing out so much about today. I really think he likes you."

"My point is that sometimes we're really mean to people we love because feelings can be so extreme."

She leans forward, elbows resting on her knees and her head on her hands. "So you love him then?"

"I'm not talking to you about this."

"Why not? Who am I going to tell? Besides, I think it's great you guys are old and finding love again."

"Watch it," I warn.

"Tell me and I promise I won't say anything."

She's so half-Sabrina—the devious half. I remember all too well the things she was able to get out of me because of conversations like this.

"It's getting late and you need to get to bed."

"Are you staying here tonight?" she asks.

I see right through this one too, Morgan.

"I am, but you know that's because I would never leave you three in the house alone. Nice try, pumpkin." I tap her nose with a smirk.

"Ugh. I hate when you call me that."

"I know, but you're so cute."

"Whatever." Morgan rolls her eyes. "I'm going to bed."

"Goodnight, honey. Listen, if that boy isn't able to be nice in front of others, then he's not worth your time. People show you who they are when others are around. Know what I mean?"

Morgan nods. "I get it. Goodnight."

She gives me a hug and then heads off.

All the kids are in their rooms and I feel very out of place. Do I go to his room? Do I get changed? This is so weird. I take a deep breath and head to Ian's room. I'm likely to fall asleep and the last thing I want is him thinking I was on the couch because I didn't want to be here. Which is its own problem since I really want to be here.

I want him.

I want to be with him.

I want to thank him for everything today.

More than anything, I just want to be in his arms.

I grab my phone and send him a text.

Me: Kids are in bed. I'm exhausted so . . . your bed or couch?

He responds not even ten seconds later.

Ian: In my bed . . . where I want you.
   Me: Is that so?
   Ian: Damn right it is.
   Me: I'll probably be asleep by the time you get here.
   Ian: I don't care. I just want you next to me.

My pulse quickens and I smile.

Me: You're being awfully sweet lately.
Ian: No, I'm just acting the way I should've with you. I'll see you soon.
Me: Be safe. See you soon.

I don't have anything sexy to wear in general, and I don't want to sleep in what I brought. I slide my pants down and rummage for something in his closet. In the back, there's a shirt that stands out amongst the dress shirts. Being the nosey bitch that I am, I check it out. When I pull the shirt out, I smile and clutch it to my chest. I bought him this shirt when he got the acceptance letter to UNLV. I went out to get him something to show him how proud I was.

It was cheesy, but Ian wore it that day and thanked me with a kiss on the cheek. It was the first time his lips ever touched my skin.

I remove my shirt and bra, slipping the UNLV shirt over my head.

And now I wait, but I'm so tired I might have to stick toothpicks in my eyes to stay awake.

Next thing I know, arms are around me and a leg is between both of mine, and I'm hot. Like, sweltering.

I roll over, finding myself cocooned and sweating. However, he looks so sweet. I touch Ian's face. I move his stubble between the pads of my fingers, loving the tiny prickly sensations.

It goes from soft and smooth to rough and then back again, just like us.

His eyes open slowly as he smiles. "Hi."

"Hi."

"Did I wake you?" His voice is gruff from sleep.

"No."

"You were passed out. I guess I was tired too."

My fingers moves down his neck and I rest them there. "What time did you get in?"

"About an hour ago."

"How was work?"

"Work." He smiles. "How were the kids?"

I shrug a little. "Kids."

"I love the shirt. You look good in my clothes." His eyes glimmer in the moonlight.

"Yeah?" I ask as the desire starts to build.

"You look good out of my clothes too, but that shirt..."

I was such a fool to think I could resist him. It's a miracle I did it for this long. All I want right now is to feel him in every way. My heart begins to beat so hard in my chest I worry it'll explode, but tonight, I need to be one hundred percent with Ian.

"Why this shirt?" I ask as I sit up.

"I remember when you gave it to me."

I slowly lift the hem, pulling it over my head and exposing my breasts. "You should have it back if it means that much to you."

His eyes travel from my face to my breasts, lingering there. He swallows loudly and I square my shoulders a bit.

"London." His voice sounds like it's about to crack. "We don't have to..."

"Shh." I press my finger to his lips. "We don't have to do anything, but I want to. I want you and us and I want you to make love to me, Ian."

He sits up, his hands cupping my cheeks as he comes closer to my lips. "Are you sure?"

My hand rests on his chest and I nod. "I've never been more sure of anything."

And then Ian kisses me.

This kiss is different from anything we've shared recently. The emotions I'm feeling are heightened and I grow dizzy from his kiss. Our tongues are gentle, moving with each other in the softest ways.

"God, I've dreamt of this," he says, and then his lips are moving down my throat.

"Not as much as I have."

He lays me down on the pillow and sits up on his knees. Ian pulls my panties down, tossing them to the floor.

"Do you know how beautiful you are?"

I shake my head.

"Then allow me to show you how I see you." Ian's hands cup my breasts, he kneads, and rubs his thumb around my nipple. "You're more beautiful than any other woman I've ever laid eyes on."

"Ian," I moan as he starts to flick his thumb against my nipple.

"What baby?"

"I want you," I pant. "I need you."

"You're going to have it all, but first I'm going to love your entire body with my mouth."

Yes, freaking please.

He leans down, taking the pebbled peak in his mouth and lavishing it with his tongue. My fingers glide to the back of his head, holding him there, needing him to keep going. His hand moves down my belly and he starts to mimic the movement of his mouth against my clit.

Around and around, pushing me higher until I break out in a cold sweat.

It's like he has a map to my body and is hitting every checkpoint.

He moves down my body, his tongue sliding along my skin. "I want you to come on my tongue."

My legs are tossed over his shoulders, and his mouth is on me before I can protest.

"Holy shit," I cry out as his tongue moves over my clit.

I know we did this a few nights ago, but it's a hundred times better than I remember. He moves his mouth in just the right way, sucking on the tiny bundle of nerves, pulling pleasure in a way that only he can.

My body stiffens as my orgasm begins to approach. I moan and grip the sheets, the pressure building to the point where I'm going to erupt. Then he begins to finger me, and I call out his name.

"I'm going to come," I pant.

He moans, sending vibrations through my pussy, and I start to shake until I'm at the point where it's almost pain. Ian curls his finger just the right way and I'm gone.

"Oh, God." I arch my back as he keeps going, making my orgasm go on and on. "Ian. Fuck. I can't," I mutter incoherently.

"Fucking. Incredible," he says as he climbs up my body.

"Only because it's you."

He pushes the hair off my face. "No, you're incredible all the time. Together, we're something else."

I reach my hand down, wanting to make him feel good. My hand wraps around his cock, and I begin to pump up and down. "I want you so much."

"You have me."

"I'm going to want you again. And again. And again."

He smiles down at me. "Baby, I'm going to have you every night. I'm going to make you addicted to this so you never leave me again."

I press my other hand to his face. "I'm not going anywhere."

"Good. I need to be inside of you, London. I need to feel you."

"No condom," I say, surprising myself.

"Are you sure?"

"I don't want anything else between us." I touch his face. "No more barriers. I'm safe, and I'm on the pill."

He kisses me hard, almost as though he didn't have a choice in the matter. "Nothing else will be between us, baby. Nothing."

Ian's cock lines up at my entrance and I close my eyes.

"Look at me," he commands.

I obey. I couldn't look away if I wanted to. In his gaze, I see everything he's feeling. Regret, desire, hope, and then, right before he pushes inside, his eyes fill with love. A love that two people shared what feels like a million years ago.

One I thought was gone forever.

"London." He says my name like a prayer. "Do you feel that?"

I nod. "I feel everything."

I never would admit it to anyone, but hating Ian was always easier than admitting I loved him. He was the first boy I loved. And if I'm honest, he's the only man I've ever wanted to love me back. My heart would ache when I saw him with anyone else. The day he married Jolene, I cried. He was mine.

He's always been mine.

Right now, I'm his.

Ian pushes deeper inside me, and his voice is deep and husky. "You feel like home."

Tears fill my eyes, blurring his gorgeous face. It's too much.

"Am I hurting you?" he asks.

"The opposite."

My hands cup his cheeks and I pull his mouth to mine. Tears run down my cheeks as I kiss him. Every emotion I ever locked away comes flooding forward and I feel each one ten times stronger than when I'd locked it up. I can't contain it any longer.

I'm irrevocably in love with Ian Chase.

CHAPTER SIXTEEN
London

"London," my boss snaps from across the conference table. "Are you even listening to me?"

I straighten up in my chair and refocus on my laptop screen. The truth is I have not been listening to him for at least the last five minutes, and I was probably only half-listening for the hour before that—actually, make that the last month. "Sorry, Casey." I clear my throat. "You were saying?"

"Christ, London. You've been so distracted lately, I don't even know what to do with you. And you're late all the time now too. Or you're leaving early. Is there a problem I need to know about?"

"No. No problem." Quite the contrary, in fact. Since Ian and I have been—I don't even know what to call it . . . dating? Sleeping together? Playing house? Whatever—I've never been happier.

"Then would you mind paying attention to what I'm saying and not staring off into space like my goddamn sixteen-year-old daughter when I'm talking to her? I get that she couldn't care less about what I have to say, but you're still looking at a promotion this year. If you want my full recommendation, you'd better at least do a better job pretending to give a fuck."

I frown. "I'm sorry. You're right."

But the moment he starts to drone on about the economic

impact of lower energy prices on the gaming industry in certain states, my mind starts to wander again.

To Ian's lips. And his eyes. And his hands. And his voice. To the way he curls his body around mine when he crawls into bed with me after work. To the way he kisses me goodbye in the morning before I sneak back to my house, tiptoeing across the lawn with a grin on my face.

I've been showering and dressing for work at home, but I go back to Ian's to help him get the kids off to school before going to the office, which is why I've been coming in late. Ian always has a cup of coffee waiting for me when I return. He kisses me hello, as if we haven't spent the entire night in each other's arms, and we share a secret smile that leaves me a little breathless. Or maybe it's his messy hair leaving me breathless. His bare chest and low-slung pajama pants. He's got that V thing that peeks out above the drawstring waist, and the sight of it sets off a massive wave of butterflies in my stomach.

Sometimes he whispers in my ear about what my high heels are doing to him—or my pencil skirt. He loves the pencil skirts. We work alongside one another in the kitchen, serving breakfast, packing lunches, filling water bottles, signing permission slips, double-checking homework, going over the afternoon schedules, hurrying the kids out the door. It's noisy and chaotic and sometimes difficult when one child or another is slow to get moving, or refuses to drink their juice, or realizes at the last second they forgot to tell us they need money for a field trip/canned goods for the homeless/a Betsy Ross costume for a book report. But it's a lovely kind of chaos, and Ian and I handle it together. Lately, I've been driving the girls to school while he drops Christopher off just to save a little time. Sometimes we manage one last kiss on the cheek before racing out the door, and sometimes we barely exchange a parting glance, but it's okay. We're making it work.

"London, for God's sake."

I snap to in time to see Casey roll his eyes at me. "Ah. Sorry. I missed that. Can you repeat the last part about regulatory reform?"

He sighs loudly. "You know, I haven't mentioned this, and maybe I shouldn't because you're not doing much to build my confidence in you lately, but there's an even bigger spot opening up if we get that Atlantic City hotel and casino account."

"There is?"

"Yes. I even thought about putting in for it."

"What is it?"

"CFO."

I suck in my breath, and my pulse races. "Really?"

He nods. "But it's a lot of responsibility. And until a couple weeks ago, I'd hardly have hesitated to recommend you. Your credentials are excellent, and your performance here has been stellar. Your work ethic is exemplary, and your conduct has been professional."

Pride fills me. "Thank you. I work hard, so that means a lot."

"But," he continues, ignoring my comment, "if I'm going to throw your name in the ring, I need to know you'd give this job a hundred and ten percent. Corporate won't stand for any half-assed or distracted efforts. If you've got personal issues of some kind that are going to get in the way of your career..."

I bristle. "I don't."

"Good. I've always thought you had a good head on your shoulders. You're not like a lot of women."

"What's that supposed to mean?" I explode.

"Calm down. It was a compliment."

"Jesus Christ, Casey." Although, it's not like I'm surprised. The corporate world is full of men—even well-meaning men—who make clueless, insulting comments like that all the time.

"All it means is that your priorities have always been lined up the right way to advance your career."

I cock my head. "Lined up the right way? Like a man's, you mean?"

"Exactly," he says, not catching my drift at all. "Most women wouldn't work as hard as you have to get ahead because they're more focused on getting married and having a family. You've moved up this far because you've never given any indication that work didn't come first for you. It's very professional."

I don't know whether to thank him or kick him in the balls under the table. What he's saying about women in general makes me angry—a woman shouldn't be held back just because she wants a family—but what he's saying about me in particular is true. I have put work first. I have focused on advancing my career. I am professional.

But at what cost?

I think about my nights with Ian, my mornings and evenings with the kids. I've never had that. I didn't even have brothers and sisters of my own. My mother was a showgirl who ran off with some tourist when I was four. I was raised by my dad, who was quite a bit older than my mom and much more introverted. Our house was quiet and organized, and I spent a lot of time alone there because he worked such long hours. I loved being at Sabrina's, because her mother was always there, fussing over her children, homemade cookies were always in the jar, and Ian was always around to tease us. Being at his house in the mornings reminds me of those days.

"Look," Casey goes on. "All I'm saying is that it would be good to keep your head in the game. It might take some sacrifice, but the potential payoff is big. You don't want to fuck up this opportunity, not after you've come this far, do you?"

"No," I say. "I don't."

"Good. Because there are others I could recommend for the job, London. You're not the only qualified candidate. There's Martin, and—"

"I get it," I say through clenched teeth.

"Good. Then let's go over those reforms once more. Pay attention this time."

We finish up the meeting and I'm successful at focusing on the data for a couple hours. By the time we wrap up, it's after five o'clock. "Casey," I ask as we shut down our laptops and rise to our feet. "I'm curious why you decided not to apply for that CFO position yourself if the potential payoff is so big."

He shrugs as he pushes open the conference room door. "I'm in my fifties. I'm too old and set in my ways to relocate. And my wife would kill me if I said we had to move."

I stop and stare at him. "Move?"

He's still holding the door for me and looks impatient. "Yes. To Atlantic City. That's where the job is. Are you going to spend the evening in the conference room or are you coming out?"

I move forward and the door swings shut behind me. "Would the move be mandatory?"

Casey gives me a strange look. "Of course it would. That's where Corporate is. You can't be a CFO from a remote location."

"Right." My stomach is balling up.

"Would the move be a problem for you?" He's looking at me curiously. "I assumed you'd be up for it. It's not like you're married or have a family to consider. Was I wrong?"

"No," I say quickly, unwilling to blow my chances even though the thought of moving across the country has me reeling. "Not necessarily. I'm just... surprised."

"Good. I'll let you know what I hear." With a brisk nod, he heads for his office and I walk on rubbery legs toward mine. Once inside, I close the door and lean back against it.

Atlantic City. It fucking figures.

I tell myself not to panic—I haven't even been offered the promotion yet.

But the conversation with my boss has left me anxious and confused. I finish up a few things at my desk and leave work with tension heavy on my shoulders. Since graduating from college, I've been on one path, because I've had one overarching goal: become CFO of a big company in the hospitality industry. I knew it would be an uphill battle as a woman, but I'm smart, driven, and armed with degrees from prestigious schools. I never doubted I could get there, and I never let anything get in my way, least of all my personal life.

Wait, what personal life?

I frown as I pull out of the parking lot. Sabrina used to poke and prod at me all the time. *When's the last time you went on a date? You're never going to meet someone if you don't put yourself out there. It's been five/ten/fifteen years, London. Ian's moved on—it's time for you to do the same.*

I'd laugh at that. *Don't be ridiculous,* I'd tell her time and time again. *Just because I don't date very often doesn't mean I'm not over Ian. I can't stand him! I'm just busy, okay?*

The look on her face would tell me she knew the truth, but she never pushed me.

"God, I miss you, Sabrina." I say the words out loud as my eyes well up with tears. "And I need you more than ever."

As soon as I get home, I sit at the kitchen table and take out my laptop. Maybe it's ridiculous to keep emailing her, but I feel like it helps me to share my feelings with her this way. She still feels like part of my life. Eli wanders over to me and rubs against my leg, as if he knows I need a friend. I take a moment to scratch behind his ears the way he likes. "You're a good boy, Eli. But I really need my bestie right now."

Swallowing the lump in my throat, I open the screen and start to write.

Dear Sabrina,

You always said I spent too much time at a desk, but I've been happy concentrating on my career. I'm good at it. It gives me confidence and validation and purpose. Have I been lonely over the years? Sometimes. But I've taken solace in the fight to get ahead, in the knowledge that I know exactly who I am, what I'm doing, and where I want to be. The sacrifices have all been worth it.

So far.

Suddenly I feel like the path I'm on has led to a fork in the road,

and I have to choose whether to keep working toward my professional goals—no matter the price—or admit that what I want out of life has changed and go in a new direction.
Toward a life with Ian and the kids. A family.

I realize I've been holding my breath and let it out in a whoosh. Then I keep typing.

I can see it so clearly, how happy we could be together. But is that even a possibility? We're having fun, but what if that's all we're doing in his eyes? It's not like we've made any plans or promises. What if he doesn't want me forever?

My hands begin to tremble and the screen blurs because my eyes have filled with tears, but I go on.

I feel like I'm having an identity crisis. And I've got so much invested in my career—time and money and self-worth. I don't want to risk everything I've struggled for just to be hurt and disappointed again. What if I make the wrong choice?
I want to know how Ian feels, and what he's thinking about the future. But . . . it's only been a month. Granted, this thing between us started nearly twenty years ago, but he might think I'm crazy to ask where he sees it ending up. For God's sake, his divorce has only been final for a year! And you told me he vowed he'd never get married again. Do I want to turn down a huge promotion just to be his girlfriend for the rest of my life? It's not like I'm 25 and can wait around—I'm 35, and if I want kids of my own, I need to have them soon.
But he's the only man I've ever loved.
I'm so scared. I wish you were really here so I could cry on your

shoulder and hear you tell me everything is going to be okay no matter what. That I'm going to be okay.

I don't know what to do. Help me.

Choking back sobs, I click send, close the screen, and go upstairs to change. As I undress, I glance out my bedroom window at Ian's house. He's standing at the grill, his new favorite thing, which is giving off smoke. He's also laughing at something one of the kids has said. I can see Morgan standing on the diving board and Ruby dog-paddling around in the shallow end of the pool.

I want nothing more than to throw my suit on, go over there, and join them. I want to open a bottle of wine and pour a glass for each of us, let it take the edge off this day. I want to help him prepare dinner, then sit down around the table and eat like we're a family.

It scares me how much I want all that. It scares me so much that I tell myself not to go there tonight, not to depend on him always wanting me there, not to get used to feeling like I belong there, or like he belongs to me.

But I can't stay away.

Five minutes later, I'm crossing the lawn, barefoot in my swimsuit, inhaling the delicious scent of whatever Ian has on the grill. He sees me coming, and his face lights up.

"Hey, gorgeous, I was wondering when you were going to get here." He sets down the large metal tongs in his hand and comes to kiss me hello. "How was your day?"

"Fine." I try to smile back.

"Fine?" He eyes me critically. "Doesn't look that way. What's wrong?"

I attempt a wry laugh. "I didn't realize I was so easy to read."

"I know all your expressions by now, babe. This one says, 'I had a bad day but I don't want you to know it.'"

Exhaling, I shrug. "That's more or less it."

"Aunt London, watch me!" Morgan shouts from the diving board before executing a perfect forward flip into the pool.

When she surfaces, I applaud and yell, "Great job!"

Ian is still looking at me. "Tell me what happened today."

I wave a hand dismissively. "It's nothing. My boss was being kind of shitty, but I'm used to it."

"Shitty how?" He's frowning, and his chest is puffed up like he might want to go kick my boss's ass. "Did he say something to you? Or harass you in some way?"

"No, no. It was nothing like that." I shake my head. "You know what, it was nothing at all. Just a bad day. I feel better now that I'm here."

"Good. Can I get you a glass of wine?"

A genuine smile stretches my lips. "What does *this* expression say?"

"It says, 'Ian Chase is a fucking god among men.'"

I roll my eyes. "Good Lord, your ego is massive."

He smirks. "Almost as big as my—"

"Uncle Ian! Aunt London!" Ruby yells from the diving board just as I put a hand over Ian's mouth so the kids don't hear him brag about his dick.

Laughing, he grabs my wrist and turns me toward the pool, embracing me from behind. "We're watching, Rubes!"

She takes a deep breath and runs off the end of the board, doing a little ballerina twirl in the air before landing in the water. "Beautiful!" I call out when she comes up. "Very graceful."

Ian kisses my temple. "Be right back."

I miss his arms around me as soon as they're gone.

CHAPTER SEVENTEEN

ian

In the kitchen, I grab a bottle of white wine from the fridge, pull the corkscrew from a drawer, and open it up.

Mondays are currently my favorite day of the week. The club is closed, and while I used to go in anyway to do paperwork and inventory, now that the kids live with me, I don't. Instead, I trained Toby to do inventory, and assigned the paperwork to Drea. I wish there were other nights I could blow off the club completely, but as good as Toby and Drea are getting, most nights I've had to at least put in an appearance.

London has stepped up for me every time. I don't know what I'd do without her.

As I pour two glasses of chenin blanc, I wonder what happened with London's boss at work. Something tells me it wasn't just a bad day—London isn't easily flustered, especially when it comes to her job. Maybe later, after we got the kids to bed, I'll ask her about it again.

I put the wine bottle back in the fridge and head outside. "Here you go," I say as I hand her the glass.

"Thanks."

"Well, we all know how you love your wine," I joke.

London rolls her eyes. "I love you when I have wine, so I guess that explains why you keep bringing me alcohol."

Please, she loves me drunk, sober, and when I'm buried between her legs. "The lies you tell yourself."

"You think I love you?" she challenges.

"I know you do."

London pulls her head back. "Really?"

Fuck yeah, I do. I see the way she looks at me. I know she rushes over here for just one more minute together. There's not much that either of us do right now that would dispute the fact that we're both falling—hard.

"Do you?" I decide to ask instead of assume.

She takes a sip of her wine, seeming to think it over. "I don't know, Ian. I know I feel very strongly about you."

Yeah, that's what every man wants to hear. "We don't have to turn this into a serious conversation." I decide to give her the exit strategy. "I know you had a tough day, I was just being a dick and trying to make you say it."

"No." She places her hand on my wrist. "I'm not trying to avoid this because I had a shitty day at work. I mean, I think we've done really well at being honest since we've been together. I don't want to stop that. We're having fun, and that matters to me. Do you love me?"

Fucking hell. My palms start to sweat and my mouth opens and closes. *Gather up your balls, Ian, and tell her how you feel.*

Instead, I take the pussy way out. "We're having fun, raising the kids we love, and there's no need to label it, right?"

I mentally slap myself—hard. I'm such a fucking fool, but I've been here before. I've loved London and lost her. My brilliant way of getting over that was to marry a viper and have that bitch's fangs stuck in my neck, sucking the life out of me for a long time.

There's no way I'm jumping in both feet and getting taken under again.

Not happening.

"Right," she says, batting her eyes, trying to hide the hurt.

"Good. I say we just keep doing what we're doing and see where it takes us."

London forces a smile and nods her head. "Exactly what I was thinking. It's like you read my mind. Nothing serious for now, no need to really make this a thing. I mean, we live behind each other, see each other daily, so why make things complicated? I take care of things for you, drive carpool, am late to work and leave early." Her voice shifts to more angry than understanding. "I wouldn't want you to have to label anything since I'm sure that's totally not your thing. It's not like we've known each other our whole lives or that I'm basically killing myself to make life better for you and the kids, right?" She keeps going without giving me a chance to answer. "I'm just . . . doing what I can and clearly fucking it up. But you know, we'll just see where this takes us. Yup. Sounds like exactly what I want."

"Whoa!" I try to stop her. "What the hell was all that?"

"No, no, I get it. I see the writing on the wall." She sets her wine glass down.

I'm glad she does because I'm fucking lost. "What wall?"

"The wall you always put up. The one you're the king of. Humpty Dumpty and all. Only I usually take the fall."

"Have you lost your fucking mind?" I'm confused because I swear just a few seconds ago she was saying she didn't want to get into this. Now she wants to, but doesn't really want to put herself out there. I'm not sure how to salvage this. "Are you drunk? Since when do you usually take the fall? How am I the one that said something wrong by being honest?"

Well, honest while holding back a little.

Fire burns in her eyes. "Oh? I must be drunk for telling you that you're an asshole, huh? I mean, it couldn't possibly be what you've done to make me feel this way."

Clearly that was the wrong question.

"I make you feel this way?" I ask, digging the hole a little deeper. I know she's hurt because I didn't admit I loved her, but I didn't hear *her* screaming it either. She was just as non-committal as I was.

"Yes, Ian." She sneers my name. "You and your feeling that what we are is just casual!"

"What the hell did you say a few minutes ago? You said we were having fun. You said it, I agreed." I call her out.

"Don't throw my words in my face." London's voice is razor sharp.

"Oh, but you can throw mine back at me?"

"Yes! Yes I can! You do this to me!"

Okay, now she's just being a nutcase. "I made you feel this way? Me? You're screaming about some shit and all I did was agree with you! Jesus Christ."

"He can't help you here, buddy. You did this all on your own."

"Did what?"

She throws her hands up in the air. "This!"

"London, calm the fuck down. You're not even making sense. I have no idea what this is! So stop yelling at me and use your goddamn words."

"Don't you tell me what to do, Ian Chase." She says through gritted teeth and heads inside the house.

Can I turn the boat around, because we went from understanding, sweet, smiling London to batshit crazy in two seconds. That was some alien invasion shit right there. I understand that I didn't exactly fess up to the fact that I love her, but at the same time, the last time I told her that, I fucking lost her.

I. Lost. Her.

So, no, I'm not exactly jumping at the opportunity to tell her again. Maybe I'm being a pussy, I get that, but at the same time, I can't fucking survive that again.

I hear banging in the house, and my stupid mirrored windows are suddenly working against me. Damn it. I need to go in there and see if she's tossing plates or who the hell knows. She's obviously pissed at me and if there's one thing I learned from my ex-wife, it's that it is usually my fault.

The bottom line is I don't want to see London upset. I want to be the one that makes her smile.

I look at Chris, who's sitting in a chair looking at his phone. "You stay out here and watch your sisters. I'm going to . . . I don't know, walk into the lion's den, but just don't take your eyes off them, got it?"

Christopher nods. "Sure thing."

Morgan laughs. "Good luck, Uncle Ian. You're going to need it."

If she wasn't already in the pool, I'd toss her ass in right now. "You better sleep with one eye open tonight, kid."

She shrugs. "Keep Aunt London waiting and stewing and you should be doing the same. She's scary."

Of all the things that irritate me about Morgan, the fact that she's usually right about handling London is at the top of my list.

"Whatever, I'm the man of this house."

Morgan laughs. "Sure, whatever you tell yourself."

If she wasn't my niece, I would really hate her. Instead of arguing with her, I head inside where the real fight is. I brace myself for whatever wrath could be waiting as I enter, but find London standing at the kitchen island. She's foregone the glass and is drinking the wine straight from the bottle.

I really screwed up, and yet I can't tell her what she wants to hear. I thought I knew what love was once. I thought I had my shit together but I fucked it up.

I don't want to do that again. Am I a little scared? You're damn right I am. The minute I give myself permission to love her fully, and say those words out loud, there's no going back. London Parish will own me, as if she doesn't already. Hell, I'm not even sure she ever stopped owning me.

This is too important to mess up. There's no rush. We can take things slow and get it right this time.

I make my way to the island and wait. After a few second

without her even acknowledging me, I decide to start this conversation. "Look, what I said back there—"

"Don't start, Ian. Just don't."

This is going great already. "If you want to talk about us—"

Her eyes narrow and she glares at me. That whole saying if looks could kill, I'd be dead. "I don't want to talk."

I put my hands up. "Okay, I'm just trying to help here. I don't want you to be upset."

"Help? I'm drowning, Ian. Are you going to help me when I'm under water? Huh? Are you going to fix the tanking of my career?"

Okay, so her bad day was clearly much worse than she let on. Maybe this fight was not just my fault. "If you want me to, then yes."

She laughs. "Right."

Anger, I get. I was full of it for a very long time and this is the exact shit I would do. Sabrina was always my go-to when I needed a kick in the ass, now it's London. She has no problem calling me out on my shit but I have to tread carefully or she may explode again.

"Talk to me, baby," I say gently, placing my hands on her hips.

Tears fill her eyes. "I just . . . I always knew what I wanted. I had a plan, and my plan was built to give me the best opportunity at success."

"I get that."

She places the bottle down and sighs. "I didn't plan on you again. I didn't plan for Chris, Morgan, and Ruby to be this important to my entire life. I love them, I always have, but they're like my own children now. I never would've put my career on the back burner, and that's what I've done."

I pull her a little closer to me since her guard is down a bit. "Is that what happened today?"

London shakes her head. "Yes and no. I was reminded in a not-so-subtle way that over the last month, I've let my personal life overshadow the furthering of my career. I'm late, I leave early, I'm unable to complete tasks on time, and they've noticed."

This is why I could never work for someone else. I am a smart enough man not to say that to her though. I've never seen her this depressed about work. London loves her boring-ass job. For whatever reason, she gets off on all that accounting crap. I would rather be with people, but that's not her. Never has been.

She's a perfectionist and it must be eating her alive to have them point out her slips.

"What can I do?" I decide to be the man, give her support and options. I want to fix this for her, but I learned a long time ago that London will say no, even if it's the best plan ever. "Tell me how to make this better for you."

Her hand touches my chest and I watch her guard drop. "You're so sweet. Well, most of the time."

"I just want you to be happy."

"I am happy with you, Ian. You make me happy, and God, I'm such a bitch for snapping like that. I'm sorry. I'm so sorry."

And I'm the hero again. Take that, Morgan.

"Don't apologize. I've missed fighting with you."

She shakes her head with a smile. "You would."

"I do," I explain. "You're fucking sexy as hell when you're pissed off."

London's hands move up my chest. "So all those years were what? Foreplay?"

"Pretty much." I'm not ashamed to say it. I love a woman who will stand her ground, can fight back, and the fact that she's hot as fuck doesn't hurt either.

"You're such a dick." London's conviction is lacking.

"If the kids weren't outside, I'd lay you on this countertop and fuck you so hard," I tell her as my cock gets hard.

It doesn't take much when it comes to her.

London brings her lips to mine, brushing them softly but not touching completely. "I have another idea."

"Yeah?" I ask, trying to gather any self-control I have.

"Uh huh. They can't see through those windows," she

reminds me and then drops to her knees, while I look outside. "The island gives us another layer to let me blow your mind."

Then London pulls my bathing suit down and does exactly what she promised, while I thank God I came inside the house to find her.

CHAPTER EIGHTEEN
london

Three weeks later, I get the promotion.
"What am I going to do, Eli?" I ask him as he rubs against my ankle. "What the fuck am I going to do?"

The offer validates all my hard work. It means my entire career meant something. But I have to lose everything personal to have it.

Ian and I will never work cross-country. He has his club so there's not a chance in hell he's coming to New Jersey. I'm going to have to leave the kids that I love more than my own life. It's just ... impossible.

How do I choose?

How do I give up the man I love or the job I love?

My phone dings with a text.

Ian: Come over! Quick! 911!
Me: On my way!

. . .

I rush out the door, not even caring what the hell I'm wearing. I forget shoes in my haste to get there . . . and pants. "Ouch!" I yell as I step on a rock, but keep going.

As fast as I can, I pull the patio door open. "Ian!"

"Up here!"

I race up the stairs, my legs quivering in fear, and pain from the rock, to find him outside the bathroom door.

"What's wrong?"

Ian lifts his shoulders. "Where are your pants?"

"You said 911, I ran out the door!"

"In your underwear?"

Does he seriously want to discuss my lack of clothing?

"Focus. What's wrong?"

"Oh." He snaps out of it. "Morgan, she's been in here a while. I called for her a few times, but she refuses to come out. Keeps crying and telling me to go away. Then, I tried checking on her a few minutes later, and she screamed at me that all she wants is her mom. So I panicked and called you right away."

Oh, God. This poor girl.

"Morgan?" I tap softly.

"Aunt London?" Morgan sniffles.

"I'm here, what's wrong, honey?"

My heart is breaking, thinking she's in pain or something is wrong, that she needs Sabrina. These are the moments there's no guidebook to help us handle.

"I'm unlocking the door," she says. "Only you can come in!"

Ian backs away so Morgan doesn't see him.

"Okay, only me."

When the door opens, I see immediately what's wrong. Morgan got her period for the first time. Her eyes are red from crying so hard, and her clothes are in the sink while she's wrapped in a towel.

"Don't be scared," I tell her quickly.

"I . . . I don't know what to do . . ."

"I know. It's going to be okay, you're just becoming a

woman." I touch the side of her face. "I'm going to get you clean underwear and shorts. You just stay in here, and I'll help, okay?"

She nods. "I didn't want to tell Uncle Ian and I didn't have my phone."

"Shh," I tell her. "We've got this."

The first time a girl gets her period always seems go one of two ways: not a big deal, or a total horror story. Unfortunately, Morgan's will be one of those horror stories.

I exit the bathroom, and Ian is right there.

"Is she—"

My finger touches his lip and I tilt my head, instructing him to follow me.

When we get into Morgan's room, I keep my voice quiet.

"She got her period."

"Oh God. I'm so not equipped to handle this shit."

Yeah, we're well aware of that. However, he has to pull it together. "You need to go to my house and get a maxi pad out of my cabinet," I tell him.

Those cartoons where the eyes fall out of the character's head? It happens before me. Ian's lips part and he's just staring.

I snap my fingers in front of his face. "Hello?"

"No."

"No?"

He shakes his head. "Nope. I'll do the boy shit, but you've got the girls."

"Umm, that's not how this works."

"I'm not going rummaging through your medicine cabinet to look for pads and tampons."

I cross my arms. "Are you going to go in the bathroom and explain to her how to use them or would you rather go get the stuff so your twelve-year-old niece doesn't feel worse about herself?"

"I'd rather talk to Christopher about hair on his balls and the proper use of deodorant," Ian replies.

Well, I'd like a lot of things too, but he's going to man up and do what is required of him.

"Ian, I don't have time to argue, your niece needs you," I say like a coach would to his player. "Now, get your head in the game and go get a maxi pad from under my cabinet."

He glares at me, clearly not enjoying the situation he finds himself in. Oh well, it's not like I'm excited by this either.

"Right now, I'm cursing my sister for dying."

"Curse her as you walk your ass over there."

He leaves the house, and I head back inside the bathroom. Morgan and I talk about growing up and what all this means. She cries a lot, hating how she feels and the lovely side effects of becoming a woman. It sucks, and as much as I want to paint this into a beautiful picture for her, I'm coming up short.

Sabrina would've been so much better at this.

A few minutes later, Ian knocks on the door and slips me the pad. He brought all four options from my cabinet. After she's all cleaned up, she heads right to her room, too embarrassed to look her uncle in the eye.

"Is she okay?" he asks.

"She will be."

"Thank fuck you live right next door. I seriously thought some apocalyptic shit was going on inside that bathroom."

My stomach drops as the reality of my situation slaps me back in the face. We need to talk, and it's the last thing I want to do right now.

Ian and I are happy. I want so badly for us to work, and there's no way we'll be able to once I take the promotion.

Which is the other half of the issue—I don't want it.

I don't want to walk away from him and the kids. I don't want to know what it's like to live without him again. We didn't work out before, and maybe that was a good thing because it led us to this place. Now I'm going to have to choose to leave it or walk away from everything I've worked for.

"She's fine, Ian, but we need to talk."

"Okay. Are you angry?"

"No, no, there's just something I need to tell you about."

I take his hand and lead him into the living room. We don't say anything as we make our way there. First, it's late and all the kids are in bed. Second, each moment I don't say anything is one more I can hold onto.

"What's going on?"

We sit down, and I close my eyes, trying to decide what I'm going to do. This decision will dictate the rest of my life. It affects four other people, though. I have to tell him and see where we go.

Maybe Ian will be great. Maybe we'll talk this through and figure out a plan that works for us. I could be blowing this all up in my head.

Wouldn't be the first time.

We're both grown-ups and this isn't the end. I know deep in my heart he loves me.

After a few seconds, Ian clears his throat. "Lon, you're scaring me."

I shake my head, bringing my eyes to meet his worried blue ones. "Don't be scared. I'm just in my head, but I want to talk to you."

"Okay?"

"I'm being crazy and I don't know why." I let out a nervous giggle.

"I don't either."

The butterflies in my stomach won't settle and I'm starting to feel clammy. "I got a promotion," I blurt out.

Ian's face lights up with pride. "That's great! You've worked your ass off for that company."

I nod. "Yeah, I have, for a long time."

"I'm glad they see how amazing you are. Not that I know what the fuck you do there," he says, chuckling.

"I'm an analyst," I say for the millionth time.

"Okay, and what would you be now?"

"Well, they want to make me the CFO."

"Holy shit, London. When would you start the new position?"

If it were up to Casey, I'd be on a plane tomorrow. "It's a great opportunity, it really is, but I'm just not sure I'm going to take it."

"Not take it?" Ian's eyes fill with confusion.

"There would be a lot of changes to our lives."

Ian wraps me in his arms, and I want to cry. All of this elation is great, but there's more. "We'll figure it out. I think the five of us have adapted well and we just shuffle things around." He kisses me and then pulls back. "I'm proud of you. I know you had a shitty day a few weeks ago because they said you weren't pulling your weight, but look at you now."

"Ian," I sigh. God, he's going to hate me.

He pulls back and then his eyes narrow. "Why aren't you happy about this?"

I take his hands in mine and nerves hit me like never before. "The job is in New Jersey."

CHAPTER NINETEEN
ian

New Jersey?

She's kidding, right?

After everything we've been through, she's going to move across the fucking country? Jesus Christ.

My mind searches for something brilliant to say, but all I keep thinking is that she's going to leave me again.

"Say something." London's soft voice is brimming with fear.

"Wow." I push the word out. "New Jersey."

"Look, I'm not happy about this. I don't really want to take it, but I'm torn. It's a great opportunity, one that probably won't come around again, but then there's us, and the kids . . ."

"I can't move there, London. The kids can't handle another uprooting like that," I explain.

"I know! I know this, which is why I'm so broken up about it. Look, I didn't want to tell you until I'd decided, but I can't lie to you, and we're a couple now. Couples talk about things like this and make decisions together."

"So you haven't taken it?" I ask.

"No, I haven't." London's eyes fill with tears. "I can't leave you. I can't do it, and as much as I want this job, and God, it's probably going to mean the end of my damn career, I don't care. I just don't. I love you. I love you and I don't know if you love me back, but I won't give up on what we have right now. Not for anything."

I try not to revert to when we were kids, but I'm right back there again. I remember it so clearly because it was the worst day of my fucking life. There I was, with the girl I had been in love with for years but never had the courage to tell, and she told me she was going to walk away from everything—for me.

The Northwestern scholarship—something only ten people in the country were offered, and she was going to walk away just for me.

How's this for some déjà vu shit again?

Now, it's a job.

Fuck my life.

"Ian, please. Say something." London lets go of my hands and wipes tears from her eyes.

"What do you want me to say?"

"Something. Anything. What you're thinking."

I'm thinking this is a sick joke the universe is playing on me. I feel like I'm in a time warp, stuck in this loop where I'm forced to give her up time after time. Stand by silently while she walks away, angry and hurt. "I—I don't know what to think."

She starts to cry harder. "How do you feel?"

Like punching something. Like begging you not to go. Like I'm about to lose the best thing that's ever happened to me. "I'm not sure."

"You're not sure?" she parrots, her voice rising. "Are you saying you don't love me?"

"I didn't say that." Because seeing her cry is going to weaken me, and I know what I have to do, I stand up and walk toward the window, shoving my hands in my pockets. "I just need a moment to think. You sprung this on me out of nowhere."

"I'm sorry. I should have told you about it sooner, but . . . I was actually hoping I wouldn't get it."

"How long have you known about it?" I ask. Does she hear the tremor in my voice?"

"About three weeks."

I spin around and face her. "Three weeks? You've known a transfer to New Jersey was a possibility for three weeks and you never said anything?"

She rises to her feet, fresh tears spilling. "I'm sorry! I wanted to, honestly I did, but we were so happy, I couldn't bring myself to do it. I didn't even like thinking about it."

"Problems don't go away just because you refuse to think about them. I shouldn't have to tell you that."

"You don't." Her voice breaks over a sob, and it kills me not to take her in my arms. God help me, I want to so badly.

I want to tell her the truth—that I love her and don't want her to leave, but it would be so unfair. She's worked too hard to give up her career now. My chest is painfully tight. "If you loved me, you wouldn't have hidden this from me."

She shakes her head. "I didn't hide it!"

I turn toward the window again so she can't see my face. "You should take the job."

"What? No!" She comes over to me and puts a hand on my shoulder. "Ian, please. Talk to me. Why would you tell me to take the job?"

I can't look at her. "Because you deserve it. You've worked all your life for that kind of title and position. It's what you've always wanted." I swallow hard and force myself to say it. "And there's nothing here worth staying for. You should go."

"But . . . but I love you. I love the kids. I love the life we're making together. You don't think that's worth staying for?"

I shrug. "Not if it means giving up your career."

Her voice is small and fragile. "Don't you love me?"

Oh, fuck. I have to lie to her. And it's going to destroy her. Crush her. Annihilate her.

But it's going to save her from making a huge mistake—if I tell her the truth, she'll pass up the opportunity of her dreams for me. Sure, she's saying she doesn't care, but I know her better than that. She wants this job, and it will be my fault if she doesn't take it. Dream over. I couldn't live with it back then, and I can't now.

No matter how much it hurts.

Turning toward her, I make myself look her in the eye. "I care about you, London. You were an important part of my sister's life, and you mean a lot to my family."

Her lower lip trembles. "That's it? After everything we've been through the last couple months, that's all you have to say to me?"

"What do you want me to say?" My gut feels like it's being torn apart by a pack of wolves. "Look, we've had a good time together, and maybe if you hadn't gotten a promotion, we'd have stayed together longer. But this was bound to come to an end sooner or later."

"It was?"

No, but that's not what comes out of my lying mouth. "Yeah." I run a hand over my hair, knowing I'm the biggest asshole in the world right now. But I have to be brutal, or she won't go. "I mean, how much longer was this going to last?"

"I don't understand." Shaking her head, she wraps her arms around herself like she's cold and takes a step back from me. "How could I have been so off about this? About us? How could I have been so blind?"

"Don't be too hard on yourself. We were having fun. We deserved it, after what happened to Sabrina and David. We needed each other to get through it."

There are no words to describe how much I hate myself right now. Saying that to her makes my heart ache because if it hurt me that much to say it, I can't imagine how it sounded.

"That's what this was for you? Grief therapy?" Her eyes are wide and shining.

"Well . . . sort of. Wasn't it that for you?"

"No. No, it was much more than that. I love you, Ian. I've always loved you. Even when I hated you, I loved you."

"That makes no sense." But it does. Of course it does.

She starts to laugh, even as tears continue to drip down her cheeks in mascara-streaked tracks. "You know what makes no sense? Me, thinking this time was different. Me, thinking you'd changed. Me, believing I could be the one you wanted forever, that we had a future together. I see now what an idiot I was."

"London, come on." Dammit, I don't want her blaming herself.

"No. You don't love me. You don't care about me. You never have." She turns for the back door, and I can't stand it.

I chase her down, grasp her arm. "Just wait a minute. That's not true."

She tries to shake me off, glaring at me over her shoulder. "Let me go, you son of a bitch. Once and for all."

But I tighten my fingers around her wrist. "You're wrong. I do care. I just see things clearer than you do. You need to take this opportunity or you'll regret it."

Her eyes narrow. "Thank you for mansplaining my life to me. Now let go."

I don't want to. Because I know that the moment I take my hand off her is the moment I lose her forever. I'll be more alone than I've ever been. And more miserable, because now I know how good we can be together.

But I have to put her first. I have to be brave enough, strong enough to do what needs to be done. That's what a man does.

I loosen my grip, and she yanks her arm away, unleashing a torrent of gut-wrenching tears at the same time.

Devastated, my throat tight, I watch her spin around and rush out the back door. She takes off across the yard without even shutting it behind her.

With my heart in a vise, I keep her in my sight until she disappears inside her house. I imagine her running up the stairs to her bedroom and throwing herself facedown on the bed to sob into her pillow just like Sabrina used to do when she was young.

Fuck, it hurts. Closing my eyes, I tip my forehead to the glass and gently bang it there a few times. *I had no choice*, I tell myself. *I had no choice.*

"Uncle Ian?"

I turn around to find Morgan there behind me, an uncharacteristically nervous look on her face. I clear my throat. "Yeah?"

"I thought I heard shouting. Is everything okay?"

Squaring my shoulders, I put on a blank face. "Everything is fine."

"Where's Aunt London?"

"She went home."

"Why?"

"Because she lives there."

Because I hurt her.

Because she's not mine anymore.

Because every time I think we can get this right, I'm forced to sabotage it.

Ignoring the little voice in my head that insisted I was choosing sabotage for my own sake, I brush past Morgan and head for the kitchen. Lately, London and I have been packing lunches for the kids the night before. It makes the mornings less hectic, and right now I need something to do with my hands or I might put a fist through the wall.

Morgan watches me take out slices of bread, peanut butter and jelly. "Doesn't she usually help you with the lunches?"

"Why don't you help me tonight?"

She doesn't answer right away. It's clear she knows something is off. The little shit is so perceptive, just like her mother. "Okay."

I hand her the butter knife and the jar of Skippy. "Here. You do that while I get the drinks."

In the pantry I grab two small bottles of water for her and Chris and a juice box for Ruby. While I'm shoving them into their lunch bags, Morgan glances at me. "What are you mad about?"

"I'm not mad."

"Yes, you are. I can tell."

"Fine." I go over to the fridge and yank it open. "I'm mad because nothing I do seems to turn out the way I want it to."

"What didn't turn out?"

I grab a few snack packs of carrots and ranch dressing and stick them into the bags. "It's complicated, okay? But I had to make a tough decision."

She nods slowly and puts the sandwiches she's made into small Ziploc bags. "Did someone have to get hurt?"

"Yes." I brace myself on the counter and exhale. "But it had to happen. There was no other way."

"Uncle Ian, I—"

"Go back to bed, Morgan." I straighten up and stand tall above her. "This has nothing to do with you."

"But I—"

"Go!" I roar, hating myself even more for being rough on her. This wasn't her fault. But I couldn't let myself soften, or I'd be lost.

My niece bites her lip, and for a moment, I think she's going to burst into tears and run away. But she doesn't—incredibly, she rushes toward me and throws her arms around my waist, pressing her cheek to my chest. It's exactly the kind of selfless, affectionate thing her mother would have done.

At first I'm so stunned, I just stand there like a dummy. A lump forms in my throat. My heart aches. My eyes burn. But she holds on tight, and after a moment, I wrap my arms around her and hug back. Somehow this twelve-year-old knows me better than I know myself.

That's why I'm grateful she doesn't ask any more questions before she goes up to bed.

When she's gone, I finish making the lunches, stick the bags in the fridge, and turn off the lights. When I crawl beneath the sheets, I reach over to the other side of the bed, even though I know it's empty. Hour after hour passes and I can't sleep, my mind full of memories, my heart full of sadness. I keep telling myself I did the right thing, but it doesn't make me feel any better.

I fucking miss her already. I always will.

CHAPTER TWENTY
London

I stumble home with hot tears streaming down my face and huge, gasping sobs wracking my chest. Somehow I manage to get up the stairs to my bedroom, even though I'm crying so hard I can barely see, and I throw myself across my bed and weep until my eyes run dry.

Why does this have to hurt so much? Why was I stupid enough to open my heart to him again? Why didn't I learn the first time that Ian Chase will never love me the way I love him?

It feels like hours that I lie there choking on my regret. Eventually, I haul myself off the bed, get undressed, and throw on a ratty old T-shirt. I skipped dinner tonight, but I'm not hungry. I have an open bottle of wine in the fridge, but I don't want it. I should wash my face and brush my teeth and take my pill, but I can't find the energy. Instead, I crawl beneath the covers, curl into a ball, and squeeze my eyes shut.

I don't want to think about him anymore. I want to be strong. I want to push through this. I want to be the kind of woman I've always admired, the kind that learns from her mistakes, stays focused on her goals, and doesn't let anyone get to her.

"Damn you, Ian," I whisper into the dark. "You made me need you, and I never wanted to need anyone ever again. You made me break a promise to myself that I'd never trust someone like you. You made me forget what it was like to have a broken heart."

I make my decision—I'm going to take the job. I'm going to show Ian that he doesn't have the power to hurt me anymore. I'm going to move to Atlantic City and make a new life for myself. I'll miss the kids terribly, but it's what I have to do. Sabrina would understand.

If I stayed here, where I'd have to look at his house every day and remember how close I came to having it all, I'd fall apart.

I have to go. He's left me no choice.

~

The next morning, I inform Casey that I've decided to accept the offer.

He smiles confidently. "Of course you accepted it. Only a fool would turn down an opportunity like this, and I know you're no fool."

Don't be too sure, I think to myself. "When should I plan to head out there?"

"As soon as possible. Have your assistant book a flight for tomorrow if she can. Take today to tie up loose ends here and get the paperwork taken care of."

"I'm traveling first class," I state flatly, daring him with an icy stare to deny me.

He nods. "Whatever you want."

What I want is to stay here and raise a family with Ian. If I can't have that, I can at least demand to be treated with the respect I deserve at work. It's all I have now.

I spend the rest of the day packing up my office, on the phone to Atlantic City getting details about the new position, and writing emails introducing myself to my new team. The contract is faxed over that afternoon, and I notice they've even included the hefty bonus I asked for, which I figured they'd reject. I would also get corporate housing in a luxury condo until I could find something more permanent, a company car, and an expense account that made my eyes pop.

In every way, this promotion was a dream come true.

It just wasn't my dream anymore.

My assistant gets me on a flight for the following morning, and at the end of the day, she gives me a hug and tells me she'll miss working for me. We carry a few boxes out to my car, and I drive away from the office for the last time, feeling oddly empty and unemotional.

When I get home, I find a note taped to my front door. For a moment, my heart races hopefully. Could Ian have come to his senses? But when I unfold it, I discover it's not from him.

Aunt London, please come over as soon as you get home. I need to talk to you.

Love, Morgan

I don't even think twice. When one of those kids needs me, I have to be there. And I want to tell them about the job myself. I need to explain why I'm moving across the country and reassure them I love them and I'll still be in their lives.

Without even bothering to change out of my suit, I go out the back door, cross the yard, and head around the house with the note in my hand. It's been a while since I've knocked on Ian's front door, but I don't feel right just letting myself in the back anymore.

I knock three times and hold my breath, willing my face to remain neutral in case Ian answers. But it's Morgan who pulls the door open. She looks happy to see me.

"Hi," she says. "Come in."

I hesitate. "Is your uncle here?"

She shakes her head. "He's picking Ruby up from dance."

Disappointment and relief all at once. "Oh. Okay."

I follow her up to her room, where she sits cross-legged on the unmade bed. Dropping down next to her, I cross my legs. "How did it go today with . . . everything?" I glance toward the hallway bathroom where she'd been in crisis mode last night.

"Oh! Fine. Everything with that was fine. The housekeeper got me some things this morning."

"Good." Had Ian instructed the housekeeper to do so? That was thoughtful of him. My heart softens traitorously toward him.

"Aunt London," Morgan begins, her eyes drifting sideways. "I have to tell you something."

I put a hand on her knee. "You can tell me anything. Always."

She takes a breath and meets my eyes. Hers are tearful. "I heard you and Uncle Ian last night. I know about the job offer and the move to New Jersey. I know everything."

"Oh." For a moment, all I can do is blink at her. "Oh."

"I'm sorry, I didn't mean to eavesdrop, but I was coming downstairs to ask you something, and I heard you talking in the living room." She wipes her eyes.

"It's okay, sweetie." I reach for her. "Come here."

"Don't go!" she bursts out. "Please don't leave us!"

My throat closes up and I'm on the verge of breaking down too, but I tell myself to be strong for her. "Oh, honey. I'm not leaving you. I'll always be in your life."

"But we need you here," she wails.

"You'll have your Uncle Ian here," I say gently. "Your mom and dad wanted you to live with him."

"I know, but—but—how can he just let you go? He loves you, I know he does!" She continues to sob on my shoulder as I rub her back and realize that even when your heart is already in a million pieces, it can shatter again.

"Well, it's hard to say." I give up fighting against tears, and weep along with her. "Your uncle and I have a lot of history, and our feelings for each other are complicated because of it."

"I don't understand."

"Of course you don't. You're not old enough yet."

"Please, Aunt London." Morgan sniffs and pulls back from me. "Don't treat me like a baby. I'm a woman now."

It almost makes me laugh, but I'm careful to hide my smile. "Okay. Well, once upon a time, when I was about your age, I developed this huge crush on my best friend's older brother."

"Uncle Ian?"

I nod. "Yes. Have you ever had a crush on someone?"

"Not really. My best friend Sarah has an older brother, but he's disgusting."

I give in to a smile. "Give it time. You might see him differently someday. Anyway, for years I had this crush on Ian, but whenever he looked at me, he just saw his little sister's friend. And then one day . . ." I close my eyes, and a shiver sweeps over my skin. "He saw more."

"What happened?"

I open my eyes and look at her. She's too young to hear the whole truth, but she deserves to know why things between Ian and I were so fraught with tension. "He took me to the senior prom. We spent some time alone together, and we said something to one another that made me believe I could be what he wanted. I was ready to change my entire life for him—I was even going to turn down my scholarship to Northwestern University."

"But you didn't?"

"No. Because later that very day, I realized that I hadn't meant anything to him. He hadn't meant what he said to me. He wasn't a bad person," I said quickly, not wanting her to think ill of the man she had to trust to take care of her, "but to me it was clear that he didn't feel the way I did. I was heartbroken."

"So you left?"

"Yes." Tears spill from my eyes, the wound opening up. "I'm sorry, honey. This is ancient history, and it's silly to cry over now."

"I don't think it's so ancient. I think you still love him."

"Even if I do, it doesn't matter. He told me to take the job in New Jersey. You heard that, right?"

"Yes, but that doesn't mean you should! He can't make you!" A flash of anger cuts through her sadness.

"No, he can't, but if he doesn't feel about me the way I feel about him, then I need to go. I know it's hard for you to understand, but if I stay here, I'll never get over him. I'll never be happy." I wipe tears from beneath my eyes.

She nods sadly before throwing her arms around me. "I love you, Aunt London. I want you to be happy."

We hold each other, both of us sniffling, and we don't let go until we here a door close downstairs. Morgan's nose and eyes are red and I imagine mine are the same. I don't want Ian to see me like this.

Unbelievably, Morgan seems to understand. "I'll go down first if you want to use the bathroom."

"Thank you." I squeeze her hand. "You're so like your mom. Oh, there is something you can do for me."

"What?"

"Take care of my cat for a couple weeks? Until I can bring him out there?"

"Of course. I'll move him in here with us so he's not lonely."

"That's perfect. Ask your uncle first, though. Okay?"

She smiles and heads out of her room.

In the bathroom, I blow my nose and splash some cold water on my face. When I'm presentable, I hold my head high and go downstairs.

As I get to the front hallway, Ian is standing there. His eyes widen. "Oh, hey."

"Hi," I say quickly. This is beyond awkward.

"I didn't know you were here."

And I wish he never knew, but here we are, face to face.

I clear my throat. "Morgan asked me to stop over, and we just had a long talk. I figure since I'm here, I should talk to Chris and Ruby about me leaving for New Jersey."

Ian rubs the back of his neck. "Right. Well . . . do you think that's a good idea? They've had a lot of upheaval, I don't want to add to it. No need to stress them out about something they have a while to get used to."

If only that were true.

And does he really expect me to just pack my shit and go? To not even talk to Christopher and Ruby? I'm not an asshole like him. I want what's best for those kids. Being mean, saying awful shit, and making them feel unloved isn't my style. "I think it's necessary to do now. It's happening and I think preparing them would be the better idea."

Ian nods. "Fine, but can it wait a few days or weeks? You can tell them once it's closer."

"No, Ian, it can't. My flight is tomorrow morning."

"Tomorrow morning?" he shouts. "Well, you didn't waste any time getting the hell out of here."

I'm not going to explain myself to him. He's the one that said I didn't matter. He doesn't get to act wounded now.

"Yes. Seven AM."

He huffs. "So fuck me and the kids, huh? Just like that? No time, no warning?"

"Excuse me?" Does he not recall telling me to go?

"I guess we'll just have to figure out schedules and everything in a day since you couldn't even give us a little courtesy." Ian's voice is filled with anger.

"Well, my company wanted me out there fast, so this is what I had to do." I cross my arms over my chest, needing to shield myself from the coming fight. "I didn't think you'd give a shit based on how our last talk went."

He throws his hands up in the air. "We've been doing this co-parenting thing for months, but I guess once you got what you wanted, you just take off without looking back. Nice. Real nice for the kids you claim you love so much."

Unreal. He is absolutely unreal. As if any of this is my choice.

"What I wanted?" I snort. "You think I want this? You selfish prick! This isn't easy for me!" I step closer, remembering all three kids are home and they don't need to overhear us. "I love you. I love you so much I would've given everything up for you, but you . . . you didn't want me. So, yeah, I'm leaving tomorrow because I can't handle being here. I can't look at your back door and not burst into tears."

"Spare me the dramatics."

"You are such a fucking asshole! I don't know how I thought you were ever the Ian of two days ago. You should've gone into acting because you really sold the show."

He laughs. "Whatever you need to tell yourself."

"What was the airport then? Huh? Or what about the boating? Or when you made me feel loved? What about all the time we just spent on the couch, cuddled up, being together? Was it all just some cosmic joke for you? Some way to get back at me for something?" I fire off questions at him in rapid speed.

I hate how he can manage to make it seem as though I'm the crazy one. I didn't do a complete one-eighty here. He did. I'm the same person I've always been. Our relationship was supposed to be different this time, but as soon as he heard something he didn't like, Ian went right back to the man I always knew.

"No, Lon, the joke is all on me."

"I guess I'm just the punch line?"

Ian takes a step back. I see something in his eyes, but it's gone before I can think more on it. "It's none of my business what you do anymore. I'll get a nanny or something."

And there I have my answers. Nothing I said matters. He's made his feelings perfectly clear. I'm nothing to him other than a babysitter. He's worried about his precious club and job, not the pain he just put me through—again.

I waited my entire life to feel the way I did when I was with him. I never married or had anyone serious because no one could measure up to Ian. Then, I finally have this chance with him. He forces my defenses to lower, gives me hope, and ends up destroying me.

Fool me once, shame on you. Fool me twice, shame on me.

Loving Ian was never really a choice, though. He's always

been the guy for me. I just wish my heart knew he was the wrong one.

"I should talk to the kids now so I can get back and finish packing," I say to him, hoping he'll say something to stop me.

"Yeah, I guess you should. You and I are over, might as well make it known."

Ian delivers the final blow to my heart, leaving it decimated.

CHAPTER TWENTY-ONE

ian

I finally get Ruby to bed. She didn't take London's big news all that well. In fact, she hasn't cried this hard since she moved in with me. She kept asking over and over, "Why can't Aunt London live here? Why does she have to leave?"

Because life is full of fucked-up moments where it takes every opportunity to kick you in the nuts and watch you fall to the floor.

Because she deserves more, kid. That's why. She deserves everything I can't give her. Her dreams were always bigger than me and I'm the fucking idiot who thought maybe I could be a part of them.

"Uncle Ian?" Chris knocks on my door.

"Yeah?" I reply tersely.

I'm really not in the mood for parenting right now. I'm trying to keep my emotions under control, but I'm on the edge. I'm angry at the world, but these kids shouldn't have to see me fall apart.

He hesitates, but then steps in. "I have something for you," he says with a hint of shame in his voice. "I should've given it to you when I found it, but . . ."

"What is it?"

"A note."

My chest tightens because from the look on his face, I know it's from my sister.

"Bring it here," I tell him.

Chris walks closer, extends his hand, and gives me the envelope. When I look at the handwriting, my heart instantly sinks. My sister always wrote with these obnoxious swirls and shit. It looks like the same envelopes the lawyer handed out after reading the will. Somehow this one hadn't made it into the file with the others.

"I found it in a box we kept of Mom's. It was in a packet and . . . I didn't read it," he says quickly. "I just couldn't give it to you because I wasn't sure if I should."

"It's okay, dude. I'm pretty sure your mother wanted me to read this at my lowest point." I manage a laugh.

Sabrina couldn't have planned this any better. My nephew held this until now? Why? Because my sister is up in heaven, pulling her strings like always.

I swear, one day she'll stop meddling in my life. Although, I kind of hope she never does.

"You okay?" he asks.

"No." I'm not going to lie to him.

"Aunt London?"

Smart kid. "Yeah."

"I figured," he shrugs. "She couldn't stop crying when she told us. I wanted to ask her to stay, but I think she wants this job."

God, it's like he's inside my head. "Sometimes, Christopher, you have to let go of what you want more than anything because it's the right thing to do."

He nods as though he's got a clue what I'm saying. "So you gave her up because you love her?"

Okay, maybe he does know what I'm saying. "I don't love her." So much for the no lying. "No, I do love her, but that doesn't mean I'm good for her."

I love her more than anything, I'm just not going to be the

reason she gives things up. I want to be the one that brings things to her life.

"That's the stupidest thing you've ever said," Chris stands up and looks at me with disgust.

"Umm... wanna try that again?"

"You love her. She loves you. She's crying nonstop and you're in here pouting. I think you're scared."

"I think you should shut your mouth." I get to my feet.

"Fine. If that's what you want." He shakes his head. "Maybe you're right, Uncle Ian... you don't deserve her."

With that, he walks away and slams the door behind him.

I can't even go after him, because he's right.

Tossing the letter aside, I lie back again and fling one arm across my eyes. I can't face hearing my sister's voice right now. It will only make me feel worse, if that's even possible.

I've never felt so fucking alone.

~

An hour later, I'm still lying there when I hear another knock on the door. "Yeah?"

"Can we come in?" It's Christopher voice again.

"We?"

"Morgan and me."

I frown. Great—just what I need, those two know-it-all's coming in here to tell me I'm a coward or complain about London or bitch at me about how I'm doing everything wrong. "Go away."

"No." Morgan opens the door and strides in, stopping at the foot of the bed. She sticks her hands on her hips. "We want to talk to you."

Christopher follows her in and stands by her side, arms folded over his chest, feet planted wide.

I sit up, scowling at them. "About what?"

Brother and sister exchange a glance. "Chris and I have been talking about you and Aunt London," says Morgan.

"That's none of your business," I snap.

"We've been comparing notes," she goes on, completely disregarding what I said.

"Yeah." Christopher nods. "And we have some questions."

"This is ridiculous." I get off the bed and stand as tall as I can. "I don't answer to you. You're not the boss of me."

"Maybe we should be." Morgan's eyes narrow, and it's clear she'll take no shit from me tonight. "Chris told me what you did. You broke things off so she'd take that job. You gave her up because you love her, just like you did after the prom."

My heart thuds painfully in my chest. My face burns with outrage. "She told you about that?"

"Yes!" she snaps. "And I told Christopher, and we realized what you'd done—you broke her heart so she'd go away to school. And you're doing the same stupid thing all over again."

"You don't know anything about it." I glare at them both. "You're too young to understand."

"No, we're not," Christopher says. "We understand perfectly. You think you're doing the right thing, you think you're fixing it, but you aren't."

"Yes, I am!" I shouldn't raise my voice to them like this, but I can't help it. I feel myself coming apart at the seams. "She was going to turn down that scholarship to Northwestern if I hadn't done what I did! And she'd have passed on this promotion!"

"But that's her choice, isn't it?" Morgan challenges. "Why should you get to make it for her?"

"Because she—" I struggle to answer the question. Run a hand through my messed-up hair. "She'd hate me for this eventually. I know she would."

"How do you know?" My niece throws her hands in the air. "You've never told her the truth about what you did back then! She doesn't know you love her now! You've never given her a chance to choose you."

"I tried to tell her the truth back then, after she came home," I inform them. "She wouldn't even talk to me."

"She was hurt," Morgan says, putting a hand over her heart. "You crushed her. But you don't have to do it again."

"I know Aunt London pretty well," Christopher puts in. "And I think, more than anything, she'd hate that you're making this decision for her. You should at least tell her the truth and let her decide."

I bury my face in my hands and rub my tired eyes. My head has started to pound. When will this fucking day be over? And why is doing the right thing so damn exhausting?

Next thing I know, a hand is rubbing my back. "Stop being so stubborn, Uncle Ian," Morgan says softly. "You love her. Tell her that. Fight for her this time."

I take a deep breath and exhale slowly. "I'll think about it. Go to bed now."

They head out, but a second later, Morgan's head pops into the doorway again. "Oh, I forgot to tell you. Eli Walsh is moving in."

"Who the hell is Eli Walsh?"

She rolls her eyes at me, looking so much like my sister it's eerie. "Aunt London's cat. Jeez, get a clue already."

Then she's gone. I turn off the light, undress, and crawl beneath the covers.

All night I fight with myself about going to her house, begging her to stay, to forgive me. I lie there in agony, going over everything I said to her, everything Morgan and Chris said to me.

You love her. Tell her that. Fight for her this time.

At some point I can't take it anymore, and I march to the back door, ready to grovel, but I see her through my windows and stop.

She's standing on her deck in the moonlight, so beautiful I can hardly breathe. Her long brown hair is up in a ponytail, and she's wearing only a white T-shirt, her long legs bare beneath it. She's looking at my house. I know she can't possibly see me, but it feels like she can. I watch her watching me, then I see her wipe her cheek and walk away.

I start to go to her, but then I hear my nephew's words about not deserving her, and my chicken-shit ass freezes right where I am, in my house, wishing I was a better man.

Miserable, I walk back to bed and flop onto it, but still sleep doesn't come. Around four-thirty, I give up and jump in the shower. When I head back into my room, my eye catches the letter from Sabrina sitting there on my nightstand. Instead of putting it off anymore, I tear it open, ready for her, too, to say something I don't feel like hearing.

My dumbest brother Ian,

This is probably the hardest letter to write because there's so much to say. First, if you're reading this, both David and I are gone. I'm sure this was hard on you because I'm pretty freaking awesome. You can cry now . . . I'll wait . . .

Done yet?

Glad you got that out. Second, you are now in charge of my children's wellbeing. Don't fuck that up, big bro.

Christopher is a good kid, but he's not good at showing emotion. Watch him, please. Make sure he knows that feelings aren't bad, it's how you handle them. Give him a lot of guidance in the girl department too, his father doesn't exactly know "the moves." Lord knows you sure have that part down.

Morgan . . . I don't know what to tell you about her because she'll let you know exactly what she thinks. To be honest, that girl scares me a little. Be sure she stays away from guys like you. (Not to be mean, but let's be real, you're a heartbreaker.) However, she won't listen—because she's Morgan, so make sure that you're there to pick her up off the ground when she has her first heartbreak. I don't have to tell you that it's a pretty dramatic thing for a girl.

Ruby, my sweet little precious jewel. She's so little, and I worry that this letter will come too soon and she'll never know how much I loved her. I worry losing her parents will shape her in a way we'll never be able to understand. I think about all the things she will need her mother for and I won't be there. Please tell her about us. Show her photos, remind her that I wanted her more than anything.

You may wonder why you got them and not Mom and Dad. Well, it's because I know you. You have the greatest capacity for love. You're a kind, protective, and giving man, Ian. No matter what you try to tell yourself. There is no one in this world who has a greater opinion of you than me. I've been on the receiving end of your big heart. I'll never forget how you were always the shoulder I cried on when someone hurt me. So, now I want you to do the same for my children.

Finally, I want you to get your head out of your big ass and go to London. Tell her you love her. Tell her you were a stupid idiot who was young and thought you knew what she needed more than she did.

You don't know what she needs! She does. You love her, Ian. I know this in the depths of my soul, and guess what? She loves you too. She'll never admit that because you're a jerk, but she does.

Now that I've bestowed all my wisdom, I'm going to dry my eyes and pray you never read this. I love you.

Love,

The best sister in the entire world. You're welcome.

A tear rolls down my face as I smile. My sister was an asshole, but I loved her. And sure enough, my sister dispensed advice I didn't want to hear.

But instead of making me feel worse, it makes me feel a little better. Sabrina saw something in me. She knew in her heart I was capable of being the person the kids would need. She knew I would love and protect them forever. And maybe if London hadn't gotten that offer, Sabrina would have been right about us, too.

I toss the letter down and head into my closet. I go to grab a T-shirt only to touch the UNLV shirt that London gave me.

Why? Why is the goddamn universe trying to remind me of her and what we shared? Why can't I just give her up and not have to feel this fucking pain? I ball the shirt up and throw it across the fucking closet.

I'm doing the right thing. I know this, but I'm fucking dying here.

A car horn honks outside, and suddenly, panic sets in. My heart begins to race and everything becomes clear. London is leaving. She's going to leave me and I'll never get her back. There won't be a second chance or a return home after college. This will be the ending of our story.

I can't let that be.

I look up at the ceiling. "Okay, I get it! Thank you, Brina!"

As fast as I can, I get dressed, tossing the shirt I threw across the room on and then a pair of sweatpants. I need to get to her and stop her. We have to talk. I practically fly out of the room and barrel to the back door. She can't leave like this.

The door makes a loud bang as I throw it open, and I hear Morgan and Chris yell after me, but I don't stop.

I make it across the back lawn and into her driveway only to see a car heading away from her house.

No.

"London!" I yell as I run toward the car. "London! I'm here! Stop the car!"

I see brake lights and stop the sprint, but the car doesn't stop —it makes a left, and she's gone.

"Fuck!" I scream and sink to my knees on the pavement. "I fucked it up. I fucked everything up!"

My chest is tight from being out of breath—at least that's what I'm telling myself. It has nothing to do with the fact that I just lost her or that I don't know how I'm going to do this without her. How do you live with half a heart? How do you go on when everything you want is gone?

I stare at the corner, hating the car that took her from me, this house, her job, and myself for letting her ever get in that car. She left early, just like I should've known she would.

I broke her and now . . . I have to fix us.

In my head, I swear I hear my sister's voice ask . . . what are you going to do now, Ian?

There's only one option—I go get my girl.

I fight for her.

Pushing up off the ground, I run back to the house. All three of the kids are staring at me and I point inside. "Go! Get ready! We have to go get her!"

Morgan claps her hands and Christopher has a huge smile.

"Don't just stand there!" I say as I get closer.

"Right! Yes! Let's go get Aunt London!" Morgan yells.

CHAPTER TWENTY-TWO
London

How many tears are too many?

I wonder if you can actually break your tear ducts from overuse. If so, I'm on the cusp.

I cried all night long.

I cried as I threw shit in a bag.

I cried as I stared at his door, wondering if he could feel me begging him to love me.

I cried when the stupid car came and drove away, leaving my heart in his hands.

Now, I'm crying again as I'm standing in line to get through security.

It feels as though someone is literally ripping my heart out of my chest. The pain is so intense, it hurts to breathe.

"Miss?" The man behind me taps my shoulder.

"Yes?" I glance over my shoulder at him.

When he gets a look at me, he blinks and takes a step back. "Are you all right?"

No. No, I'm not. I'm broken, hurting, feeling as though my life is over. "I'm . . . I'm not sure."

"Can I offer you a handkerchief?" He reaches inside his jacket and takes one out.

"Thank you." How sweet, he's a gentleman. Men don't normally carry handkerchiefs anymore, do they? And here's a nice man being so sweet to a crazy lady in line who can't stop crying long enough to move up.

"Are you real? Do men like you still exist?" I ask as I blot my eyes. "True gentlemen, I mean? Guys who are chivalrous when they see a woman in distress? Because I thought I knew a guy like you once, but he turned out to be a shithead."

The poor stranger purses his lips and nods, looking a bit uncomfortable. "I see."

"Do you? Because I can't see it. I've tried. He acts like he loves me and yet he just threw me away. Who does that?"

"Um, I don't really—"

"If you love someone, you hold them close, you cherish them, you give them your heart. You don't say it was never anything to begin with and tell them to take a job all the way across the country!" I blow my nose in the soft fabric and the tears fall harder. "Jesus Christ, just look at me!"

"You do seem very upset," the handkerchief gentleman says, probably sorry he tapped my shoulder in the first place.

"I'm not normally like this," I explain. "I'm a career woman who never gave two shits about men and their games. I graduated summa cum laude from Northwestern with a degree in finance. I worked my ass off to get to the position I just got, in a sea of asshole men because I'm smart. But here I am, crying because of Ian fucking Chase."

"Would you like to step out of line, miss?" The guy behind him asks.

"No!" I say a little too vehemently, my spine snapping straight. "No. I'm going to New Jersey, sir. I'm leaving, because I have no reason to stay."

"Just asking, because—"

"No one to love me," I blubber on, my posture wilting again. "No one to care. Even my cat didn't give a shit when I left him this morning. How is that for pathetic?"

Handkerchief gentleman puts his hand on my arm. "Maybe you should sit down," he suggests.

"When is someone going to love me?" I throw myself at the poor guy, a stranger in the airport, clinging to him like a weeping toddler. "When is it my turn? Have I made all the wrong choices in life? How did I get here?"

He falls back a little because of the force with which I've launched myself at him, but he rubs my back, saying it's going to be okay. Why couldn't Ian do this? Why isn't it his arms that are around me, giving me comfort?

Oh, because he's a chicken-shit asshole who doesn't know a good thing when it slaps him in the face.

"I'm sorry," I sob into the guy's shoulder, wetting his nice blue button-down shirt. "I'm so sorry."

"Uh, it's all right, but the line is really long, and if—"

"London!" A deep voice booms, echoing throughout the cavernous airport security area.

I pick up my head and sniff. I know that voice.

"London! Don't go!"

Frantically, I look around. Am I dreaming this? Have I lost my last remaining tether to reality? Or is it really Ian I'm hearing?

The crowd around me murmurs and shifts. Something compels me to jump out of the line, leaving my small suitcase behind. I shove people aside and hurdle the yellow security ropes, not easy in heels and a skirt.

"There she is!" A younger voice, female.

I spin around, my jaw dropping open. Then I clasp my hands over my mouth. Running toward me is Ian, carrying Ruby, followed by Morgan and Christopher. The kids are in their pajamas, Ian is wearing sweatpants, flip-flops, and an old UNLV T-shirt—clothing I was sure he normally wouldn't be caught dead in outside the house—and his hair is a total mess. He looks insane.

But I've never seen anything more beautiful than the sight of them rushing toward me, never heard anything as heartwarming as the sound of them calling my name, never known a feeling as deep and powerful as the love I feel for them as they reached me.

"London," Ian chokes out, setting a smiling Ruby down and leaning forward, hands braced on his knees as he caught his breath. "Thank God."

"What's going on?" I shake my head, amazed and baffled. "What are you doing here?"

"He's fighting for you!" Morgan claps her hands and jumps up and down. Even Christopher is wearing a grin.

"Hush." Ian gently pushes his niece aside and takes my hands. "London. Don't get on that plane. Don't go."

"I have to, Ian. I took the job like you told me to." My eyes fill again. "Remember what you said? 'There's nothing here worth staying for.'"

"I lied."

"What?" I shrink back a little and search his face, but it's open and earnest.

"I lied to keep you from turning down the job for me. I didn't want you to resent me for ruining your career, for holding you back."

My heart is pounding. "But I told you I didn't care about my career as much as I cared about you. About us. And you still told me to go."

Ian squeezes my hands. His eyes are glossy with unshed tears. "I know. And I'm sorry. I thought I was doing the right thing by making it easy for you to leave, but I was wrong. And I don't want to make the same mistake again."

"Again?" Something prickles on the back of my neck. "What do you mean?"

Ian takes a breath. "The first time we were together, I hurt you on purpose so you'd use your scholarship and go to Northwestern. I couldn't let you give up your education, your dream, just to stay with me. I wasn't worth it."

"You . . . you hurt me on purpose?" The truth sinks in hard and fast, a knife through the heart.

He nods miserably. "I did what I thought I had to do. But letting you go hurt me too, Lon. Believe me. I meant everything I said to you that night. Watching you walk away from me at Sabrina's party was pure torture. But I had to."

I'm beyond shocked. "All this time . . . Why didn't you ever tell me?"

"I tried, when you came back." He shakes his head. "You wouldn't listen to me."

I bite my lip, wanting to defend myself but knowing he's right. I made up my mind about him the moment I saw him at that party with another girl at his side. But if he's telling the truth, and in my gut I feel like he is, then this could change everything. "So that was all an act? Then . . . and now?"

"Yes." He moved closer and lowers his voice. "I never stopped loving you. Ever. Even when we fought, even when I pretended to hate you, even when I tried to forget you, you've always been the one."

God, I want to believe him. But I'm scared. "Don't say things you don't mean. It's not fair."

He cradles my face in his hands and looks me right in the eye. "I mean every word I'm telling you, London. I love you more than I've ever loved anyone. You've made me happier than I've ever been before. Without you, I'll be lonely and miserable for the rest of my life, hating myself for pushing you away, when all I really want to do is hold you close." He crushes his lips to mine. "Stay with me. Stay with us. Where you belong."

I don't think. I don't move. I don't even breathe. All I can do is feel. And in my heart I know this is my dream—this man, this family, this life we're building together. "Yes," I whisper, and a second later his lips are on mine, his arms are wrapped around me, and I'm being lifted right off the floor. People in the crowd cheer and whistle and applaud, and the kids hug each other and then us. I'm still crying, but the tears are happy now, and Ian is holding on to me so tight, it's as if he'll never let go.

"I love you," he keeps whispering in my ear. "I love you so much, and I'll never let you go."

Eventually, we open our arms to the kids, and even Christopher, red-faced and grumbling a little, lets us include him in one big embrace. I'm sure we look a little crazy and ridiculous, but I don't care.

I'll never forget this moment as long as I live—a happy ending to one chapter of my life, but a brand new start to another.

I can't wait to see where love will lead us.

CHAPTER TWENTY-THREE

ian

"So what happens now?" Morgan asks from the back of the minivan I still can't believe I'm driving.

"We go home." London squeezes my right hand, which she's holding in her lap.

"Whose home? Are you going to live with us now, Aunt London?" the nosy little thing wants to know.

"Um, I'm not sure." London seems a little flustered by the question, but I'm not.

"I hope so." I pick up her hand and kiss the back of it. "All that running across the back yard is getting tiresome, don't you think? I feel like a teenager sneaking around."

"Ian!" London laughs, her cheeks going beautifully pink as she glances into the back seat.

"Please. It's not like we don't know you stay the night." Christopher's tone tells me he's rolling his eyes right now, even if I can't see it.

"Seriously," Morgan agrees. "You guys are, like, so obvious."

In the rearview mirror, I catch Ruby's eye and wink at her. "Well, Lon? What do you say? Think you can live with a hot caveman, two smart-ass teenagers, and one adorable almost-first-grader?"

London laughs, and the sound warms my insides. "I think I can handle it."

"What the heck, Uncle Ian?" Morgan shrieks in outrage. "Was that supposed to be a proposal or something? That's not how you do it!"

I meet her defiant stare in the rearview mirror. A week ago I probably would have been angry at her big mouth, but today I just grin. This is my life now, and I'm embracing every chaotic, unexpected moment. "Oh no?"

"No! You have to give her a ring," Morgan insists.

"And get down on one knee," adds Ruby.

"And maybe phrase it a little differently," my nephew suggests, the traitor.

"It's okay, you guys." London smiles at me sweetly. "Your uncle has already made me very happy this morning. One thing at a time. There's no need to rush."

But here's the crazy thing—I want to rush. I want to marry London. I want to be her husband and introduce her as my wife, and love and cherish and protect her and these kids for the rest of my life. I feel like we've spent way too much time apart already, and patience has never been my strong suit. So when I spot a billboard for the Love Me Tender Wedding Chapel off the next highway exit, I quickly veer onto the off ramp.

"Ian?" London gives me a funny look. "This isn't our exit."

"It isn't?" I spy a sign for the chapel, one of those horrible all-in-one places that will supply everything from rings to a license to witnesses to an Elvis-impersonating officiant, probably all for ninety-nine bucks.

London sees it too. "Oh, my God. Ian Chase, what on Earth are you doing?"

All I can do is grin.

When I pull into the Love Me Tender parking lot a couple minutes later, my heart is pounding. I turn off the car, turn around and look at the stunned faces in the back. "Well? Are you going to help me do this right?"

Morgan recovers first and beams. "Get out of the car. You too, Aunt London."

London, who looks like she's in shock, does as Morgan says. A minute later, all five of us are piling into the chapel's lobby, which conveniently contains a glass display case featuring some gold wedding bands of dubious quality. Nothing even remotely resembles the engagement ring I'd have chosen for London, but I can remedy that later. I take her hand and whisper in her ear. "Pick out the one you like, sweetheart. I'll get you a diamond eventually, I promise. Anything you want."

She looks at me with tears in her eyes. "Are you sure you want to do this now?"

"I've never been more sure of anything in my entire life."

She smiles. "Me either. And I don't need a diamond on my finger to prove it."

She's going to have one anyway, but I love her even more for saying that.

I grab her hand and pull her toward the chapel. "Good. Now, let's go make you my wife."

Morgan squeals. "Yes! Finally he gets his head out of his butt."

London shakes her head with a smile. "I need a maid of honor, would you be willing to stand beside me?"

Morgan's eyes widen and tears start to form. "Really?"

"Who else would I pick?"

"I would love to," Morgan says as she wipes her tears. "Mom would be so happy right now."

London's gaze meets mine and I can see the emotions swimming. "Yeah, she would."

"Enough of this sappy crap," Chris cuts in. "It's time to be happy."

"Let's go make it so London can never run away from me again," I say as I scoop Ruby up in my arms.

"Please, you don't control me."

I pull London to my side. "We'll see about that tonight."

Her lips touch my cheek and then we march into the crappy little chapel.

We fill out the paperwork, go over the questions, and London and Morgan pick out the limited decorations they have available. I stand here, staring at her, wondering how the fuck I got so lucky. I always said I wouldn't get married again. I made that mistake once, and repeating that error wasn't on my agenda, but this feels so right.

London is the person who makes my life make sense. On one hand, she's irritating, nosy, knows everything, and God forbid she's ever wrong. On the other hand, she's beautiful, funny, loving, smart, and she's usually not wrong, which brings me back full circle. I just know I can't live without her. I did that for too long, and I won't do it again.

I love her more than anything.

I need her, and now I'm going to have her.

She turns to look at me from over her shoulder, her lips quirking up into a soft smile, but her green eyes are filled with love. She winks, and then goes back to pointing into the glass case.

Chris nudges me. "I always knew you loved her."

"Yeah?"

Kids think they know everything. They don't know shit.

"You were always so angry, but Dad used to say that when you're that mad at someone, it's because you care so much you can't explain it, so you become angry."

My brother-in-law was always filled with philosophical shit, but once again, he had a point. "He might just have been right."

Chris nods. "He would tell me that after he fought with Mom."

"They fought?"

Sabrina always made it look like their marriage was perfect. He doted on her. She praised him. It was maddening because who the fuck could live up to that? Not me. They complemented each other in every way. I swear, it was scary at times. I never saw

David get irritated with her. Sabrina was always laid back and I never saw her snap at him like London does at me for things like chewing too loud.

"Are you serious? Mom was always yelling at Dad and he was great at sign language," Chris laughs. "I remember asking Dad what that finger meant and he told me it was the sign for love. So I walked up to Mom and did it. She was so pissed."

I let out one loud laugh and smile. I can see my sister not taking that well. "You know that Aunt London and I love you guys, right?"

"I do."

"Good. We're going to fight and have stupid moments. I'll probably push her in the pool a few times, and Lord knows she's going to bitch at me, but I promise you three that we'll always find a way to work it out. This wedding is sudden, but it's been a long time coming, if you know what I mean." I want these kids to know this is forever. There won't be another big disruption because London isn't going anywhere. I've loved her my whole life and now she's going to be mine.

"I get it. I think it's great," Chris says.

"One more thing." I clear my throat. "I need a best man . . . are you up for it?"

He stands a little straighter and nods. "I can do that, Uncle Ian."

I knew he could.

A moment later, London, Morgan, and Ruby are in front of us. "Are you sure? No backing out once we walk through those doors."

"There's no backing out—ever," I tell her.

London's smile grows bigger. "I love you, Ian."

"I love you."

"Mr. Chase and Ms. Parish?" The very scantily dressed lady calls us from behind the counter. "You're up."

London gives me a brief kiss. "I'll see you at the end of the aisle?"

"You're damn right you will."

Chris and I head around to the front of the chapel. It's crazy, but I'm not nervous. I keep waiting for the anxiety to kick in, but it's completely absent. All I feel is excitement and happiness. This is right and about damn time. I want to make her my wife and then take her home to consummate the fuck out of it—and her.

The music begins and Morgan walks in first. She looks so grown up. I remember when she was born, holding her in my arms, wondering what my sister was thinking, having another kid, but the first time that little girl wrapped her arms around my leg, I got it. She's always been special to me, the first niece in the family. She was always watching and observing the world around her. Then when she started talking, we understood she'd been keeping notes to give us all later.

When Morgan gets to the front, London appears, holding Ruby's hand.

I know I just saw her a moment ago.

I get that nothing has changed, but she looks even more beautiful than before.

The sun is beaming in from the window behind her, casting light all around. She's brilliant, and I don't think I'll ever forget this moment.

She continues toward me with a smile that knocks me on my ass.

"Hi," she says as she stands before me.

"Hi."

"Hi!" Ruby says and we all laugh.

"Hi, pipsqueak."

Elvis walks up to the front, and I don't even give a shit how cheesy and cliché this is. All that matters is London and me.

He goes on about love and marriage, but I don't hear a word as I stare at my bride.

"Ian." She nudges me.

Then I recall something about 'do I take' . . . "I do."

"Do you, London, take Ian for better or worse?"

"I do."

"By the power vested in me by the state of Nevada, I now pronounce you husband and wife."

I know what comes next and I don't need his permission.

I wrap my arms around her, leaning her back, and kiss the shit out of her. She holds on tight and I refuse to let go. She's mine now—and forever.

epilogue
LONDON

~ FOURTEEN MONTHS LATER ~

"Ian!" I call out. "I need a diaper!"

You would think the man would replenish the diaper holder after he uses the last one, but no, he leaves it empty so I have to stand here with crap in the baby's butt and no way to change her.

I look down at Sabrina and shake my head. "Your Daddy is a mess, Brina. A big mess. What are we going to do with him, huh?"

She's only four months old, so she just kicks her legs and smiles.

"Here!" Ian enters the room as though he just saved the world, holding the pack of diapers. "You're welcome."

"I wouldn't have had to ask if you filled them to begin with . . ."

"Yes, but then I wouldn't have had the opportunity to get told what to do, and I just love that," he says with heavy sarcasm.

"I hate you."

He laughs. "You only wish you did, baby." Then the jerkface slaps my ass.

Ian wasted no time getting me pregnant. I think he took a bet

255

with someone over how fast he could do it, because it was his damn mission. We both wanted a baby, and we both imagined time wasn't on our side. I never thought it would happen in the first month, but here we are.

"Where is Christopher?" I ask.

Christopher has started dating, he's a senior now, and he's his uncle. A ladies' man.

"He's in the game room."

"With his girlfriend?"

"Yes, why?"

I just stand there and look at him.

Ian suddenly bolts out of the room. "Chris!" I hear him yelling. "You better have your damn pants on!"

I cradle Sabrina in my arms. "You're going to be a good girl, aren't you? You're not going to like stinky boys because your daddy might just shoot one that comes to the door."

I head down to the living room where Ruby is on the couch, eating crackers and watching Frozen for the thirtieth time.

Seriously, this movie embeds itself in your brain until you're singing the words in the shower without meaning to.

"Can we go shopping, Aunt London?" Morgan asks.

In the last year, this girl has gone from semi-Tomboy to full out girly-girl. She only wears a mix of pink or teal, her hair is always done, and I think she rivals Sephora with her makeup collection. Ian was the idiot who took her shopping the first time. When they rang her up, I think he might have had a stroke because he doesn't remember actually ringing his card through.

"No, you can't possibly need anything."

She huffs. "Whatever. Brina gets anything she wants."

"She's a baby!"

I swear, this girl. When I was pregnant, Morgan was my best friend. She was always asking if I needed anything or if I was comfortable. We spoke with the kids at great length about naming her. Neither Ian nor I wanted them to be upset, and they were ecstatic that we were giving her their mother's name. Then

Sabrina came home with us, and I swear, they suddenly became completely different children.

"Still, she got new clothes!"

Thirteen is the worst age ever. I'm completely convinced.

"She outgrew them, Morgan. Stop it, seriously, you can't win this one, honey," I tell her.

"Okay," she whines, "I just was asking."

Ian appears in the living room with a scowl on his face. "That boy... is trouble."

"So what you're saying is that he's you?"

"Watch it, woman."

"You were all about training him to be your clone when Sabrina and David were alive," I remind him.

"Yes! Because he wasn't my responsibility!"

Sounds about right.

I move closer to my husband, placing my hand on his chest. "Well, that is a mistake you'll have to fix. Was he naked?"

"No, but even with my warning he was practically mounting her."

I really didn't need to know that. I can't picture that sweet boy mounting anything. I know he's older and all that, but he's still the pudgy-faced five-year-old who would sit on my lap when he came over. I can't see him as a grown up.

"Just don't leave him alone."

"They're coming up to go swimming now."

"Ian." I drop my hand. "What did we do in the pool last night because we had privacy?"

Chris was at his friend's house and Morgan was playing with the little kids. We had one of the spats that we're infamous for, and went outside to finish it up. The fight wasn't the only thing that finished, though. He said something rude and I pulled his move, shoving him into the pool. Only this time, he grabbed my waist, dragging me in with him.

After a few more words of anger, he ended up shoving his tongue down my throat.

Within minutes, I was up against the pool wall and he was reminding me what happens when we fight.

Unbelievable make-up fucking.

"Great!" Ian throws his hands up in the air and then points to Brina. "She's never dating!"

Here we go. He continues to stomp around the house and Morgan appears. "New house rule. None of you are dating anymore!"

"What did I do?" Morgan asks.

"You live," I tell her.

"You live and boys like girls. And boys convince girls to do things they shouldn't do."

Morgan crosses her arms. "You're off your meds again, aren't you?"

He turns, and for the first time, I see a bit of fear in her eyes. "No. Boys."

"Okay, fine." Her hands go up in surrender. "No boys. Got it."

"That's right, I'm in charge here," Ian informs us.

"I'm going back up to my room—where it's safe." Morgan retreats, her hands still in the air. Poor thing.

"Nowhere is safe, sweetheart," I tell her.

Ruby comes around with her arms open to Ian. "You're silly, Uncle Ian."

She is so attached to him, it's beautiful to see. He pulls her up and kisses her forehead. "I'm silly, huh?"

"Yes, because boys are funny. I'm going to be a princess and have a prince just like you."

"You think I'm a prince?"

Oh, he's a prince all right.

"Yup." Ruby squeezes him tight.

"Well, you're definitely a princess."

I smile watching them. She seems to calm him a little, and then he leans against the counter by me.

My hip bumps his. "You know you're really sweet when you're not a raging lunatic."

He laughs. "You always know what to say to make me feel better."

"I love you, Ian. Even when you're a little off your rocker."

"I love you, London. Even when you're a colossal pain in my . . ."

"Mouth!" I say before he gets it out.

Ruby told the teacher to "kiss her ass" this week. That was a fun phone call, which my husband laughed hysterically over. After two nights of him being in the doghouse, he agreed to curb his language.

"I know, I was going to say tushy," he lies and then puts Ruby down.

"Right."

"Well, I could've."

I laugh as Ruby runs back to start that damn movie over again.

"But that wouldn't make you—you," I tell him, and then move over to place Brina in her swing.

"And you love the me I am."

"For some crazy reason," I say over my shoulder.

I get her settled and walk back over to him. His arms wrap around my middle and I touch his cheek.

His lips meet mine and I melt into him. We kiss and stay in this little cocoon for a few minutes. I love that he's so openly affectionate with me. He and I haven't talked about it, but he grew up in a house where his father loved his mother. They never hid it. I remember thinking how special it was, and how much I wished I had grown up that way. Sabrina always thought it was weird and gross, but because it wasn't something I saw daily, I marveled at it.

Now, showing our kids the same level of love is important to me.

There's no doubting we love each other beyond what I ever knew I was capable of. He's the other half of my heart. Without him, I didn't know I was missing anything. I thought I had a great life, but now, my life is exceptional.

In his arms, I'm safe, loved, and respected.

We'll have ups and downs. There'll be times when things will feel as though they're falling apart, but we can weather those storms because we are meant for one another.

He wipes the tears that trickle down my face. "Why are you crying?"

"I'm just so happy."

"I am too. You make me this way."

I smile and drop my head to his chest. "Thank you," I tell him.

Ian hooks his finger under my chin, forcing me to look at him. "For?"

"Fighting for me."

"I will always fight for you, London. Even when you pull away, I'll hold you close, because this is where you belong—with me."

"Always?"

He smiles. "Always."

Thank you for reading Hold You Close If you enjoyed this book, be sure to check out other books by Melanie & Corinne that are currently available!

Including our next co-write Imperfect Match Free in Kindle Unlimited

For an EXCLUSIVE Bonus Ian & London scene ... swipe to the next page for details!

bonus scene

Dear Reader,

Thank you so much for all your love and support, and we hope you enjoyed Hold You Close! Do you want more Ian and London? If so, go to the link below or scan the QR code with your phone, sign up for our newsletter, and you'll get an email giving you access!

https://geni.us/HYC_Signup

also by melanie harlow and corinne michaels

Co-Written Novels by Melanie Harlow and Corinne Michaels

Hold You Close

Imperfect Match

Baby, It's Cold Outside (A Holiday Novella)

Books by Corinne Michaels

The Salvation Series

Beloved

Beholden

Consolation

Conviction

Defenseless

Evermore: A 1001 Dark Night Novella

Indefinite

Infinite

The Hennington Brothers

Say You'll Stay

Say You Want Me

Say I'm Yours

Say You Won't Let Go: A Return to Me/Masters and Mercenaries Novella

Second Time Around Series

We Own Tonight

One Last Time

Not Until You

If I Only Knew

The Arrowood Brothers

Come Back for Me

Fight for Me

The One for Me

Stay for Me

Destined for Me: An Arrowood/Hennington Brothers Crossover Novella

Willow Creek Valley Series

Return to Us

Could Have Been Us

A Moment for Us

A Chance for Us

Rose Canyon Series

Help Me Remember

Give Me Love

Keep This Promise

Whitlock Family Series

Forbidden Hearts

Broken Dreams

Tempting Promises

Forgotten Desires

Standalone Novels

All I Ask

You Loved Me Once

Want a reading order? Click here!

Books by Melanie Harlow

The Frenched Series

Frenched

Yanked

Forked

Floored

The Happy Crazy Love Series

Some Sort of Happy

Some Sort of Crazy

Some Sort of Love

The After We Fall Series

Man Candy

After We Fall

If You Were Mine

From This Moment

The One and Only Series

Only You

Only Him

Only Love

The Cloverleigh Farms Series

Irresistible

Undeniable

Insatiable

Unbreakable

Unforgettable

The Bellamy Creek Series

Drive Me Wild

Make Me Yours

Call Me Crazy

Tie Me Down

Cloverleigh Farms Next Generation Series

Ignite

Taste

Tease

Tempt

Cherry Tree Harbor Series

Runaway Love

Hideaway Heart

Make-Believe Match

Small Town Swoon

Co-Written Books

Strong Enough (M/M romance co-written with David Romanov)

The Speak Easy Duet

The Tango Lesson (A Standalone Novella)

Want a reading order? Click here!

acknowledgments

Our betas: Thank you for reading, giving your feedback, and coming along on this journey.

Corinne:
　　To Melanie: Thank you for taking this journey with me. I loved every second of writing this book with you. I can't wait to write many more. #joystealersbegone

To my husband and children. I don't know how you deal with me, but I can't tell you how much I appreciate you. I love you all with my whole heart.

My assistant Christy: No matter how insane I am, you keep me around. Even though I try to fire you, it never works.

My publicist Nina: You are the apple of my eye. I've had the most amazing time working with you. Thank you for making me laugh and keeping me on track.

Melanie:
　　To Corinne, for reaching out to me about writing a book together and being an awesome, supportive, talented partner. I had so much fun on this project! #irememberisaac

To Kayti, Laura, and Bethany, for always understanding me.

To Melissa Gaston, for all you do. I'd be lost without you!

To Jenn and the team at Social Butterfly, I appreciate you.

To Lauren, for the gorgeous photo that so perfectly captured our vision and our hearts.

To Nancy, for knowing what the hell we were trying to say even when we didn't.

To my husband and daughters, for putting up with my endlessly distracted mind. I'll hold you close forever.

about the authors

New York Times, USA Today, and Wall Street Journal Bestseller Corinne Michaels is the author of nine romance novels. She's an emotional, witty, sarcastic, and fun loving mom of two beautiful children. Corinne is happily married to the man of her dreams and is a former Navy wife.

After spending months away from her husband while he was deployed, reading and writing was her escape from the loneliness. She enjoys putting her characters through intense heartbreak and finding a way to heal them through their struggles. Her stories are chock full of emotion, humor, and unrelenting love.

Connect with Corinne:
Facebook: https://bit.ly/1iwLh6y
Instagram: https://bit.ly/2L1Vzo6
Amazon: http://amzn.to/1NVZmhv
Bookbub: https://bit.ly/2yc6rss

Melanie Harlow likes her martinis dry, her heels high, and her history with the naughty bits left in. When she's not writing or reading, she gets her kicks from TV series like VEEP, Game of Thrones, House of Cards, and Homeland. She occasionally runs three miles, but only so she can have more gin and steak.

Melanie is the author of the AFTER WE FALL series, the HAPPY CRAZY LOVE series, the FRENCHED series, and the sexy historical SPEAK EASY duet, set in the 1920s. She lifts her glass to romance readers and writers from her home near Detroit, MI, where she lives with her husband, two daughters, and pet rabbit.

Connect with Melanie:
Facebook: https://bit.ly/1RiTP7z
Amazon: http://amzn.to/1NPkYKs
Bookbub: https://bit.ly/2yfljWR
Pinterest: https://bit.ly/2m60beu
Instagram: https://bit.ly/2ubxh19
Website: http://www.melanieharlow.com
Stay up to date with Melanie, sign up for her Mailing List: http://www.melanieharlow.com/subscribe/
To sign up for monthly text alerts: Text HARLOT to 77948